Dedalus Europe 199
General Editor: Mike N

The Experience of the Night

Translated from the French
by Christine Donougher

The Experience of the Night

Marcel Béalu

Dedalus

Funded by
THE
ARTS
COUNCIL
OF ENGLAND

Dedalus would like to thank The French Ministry of Foreign Affairs in Paris and The Arts Council in England for their assistance in producing this book.

Published in the UK by Dedalus Ltd, Langford Lodge, St Judith's Lane, Sawtry, Cambs, PE17 5XE

ISBN 1 873982 67 4

Distributed in the USA by Subterranean, P.O. Box 160, 265 5th Street, Monroe, Oregon 97456

Distributed in Australia & New Zealand by Peribo Pty Ltd, 58 Beaumont Road, Mount Kuring-gai, N.S.W. 2080

Distributed in Canada by Marginal Distribution, Unit 102, 277 George Street North, Peterborough, Ontario, KJ9 3G9

Publishing History
First published in France in 1945
First published in England in 1997

L'experience de la nuit copyright © editions Phebus 1990
Translation copyright © 1997 Christine Donougher

Printed in Finland by Wsoy
Typeset by RefineCatch Limited, Bungay, Suffolk

THE AUTHOR

Marcel Béalu was born in the Loir-et-Cher region of France in 1908 and began his working life when only twelve. While working as a hat maker in 1937 he met the cubist poet Max Jacob who encouraged him to write.

He published the first of his seven novels *Memoirs de l'ombre* in 1941 followed by *L'Experience de la nuit* in 1945.

In his latter years he became a well-known figure as a Parisian bookseller.

THE TRANSLATOR

Christine Donougher was born in England in 1954. She read English and French at Cambridge and after a career in publishing is now a freelance translator and editor.

Her many translations from French and Italian include Jan Potocki's *Tales from the Saragossa Manuscript*, Octave Mirbeau's *Le Calvaire*, Sylvie Germain's *Days of Anger* and *Night of Amber* and Giovanni Verga's *Sparrow*.

Her translation of Sylvie Germain's *The Book of Nights* won the T. L. S. Scott Moncrieff Prize for the best translation of a Twentieth Century French Novel during 1992.

Her current projects include translating Rezvani's *The Enigma* and editing *The Dedalus Book of French Fantasy*.

French Literature from Dedalus

French Language Literature in translation is an important part of Dedalus's list, with French being the language *par excellence* of literary fantasy.

Séraphita – Balzac £6.99
The Quest of the Absolute – Balzac £6.99
The Experience of the Night – Marcel Béalu £8.99
Episodes of Vathek – Beckford £6.99
The Devil in Love – Jacques Cazotte £5.99
Les Diaboliques – Barbey D'Aurevilly £7.99
Spirite (and Coffee Pot) – Theophile Gautier £6.99
Angels of Perversity – Remy de Gourmont £6.99
The Book of Nights – Sylvie Germain £8.99
Night of Amber – Sylvie Germain £8.99
Days of Anger – Sylvie Germain £8.99
The Medusa Child – Sylvie Germain £8.99
The Weeping Woman – Sylvie Germain £6.99
Là-Bas – J. K. Huysmans £7.99
En Route – J. K. Huysmans £6.95
The Cathedral – J. K. Huysmans £7.99
The Oblate of St Benedict – J. K. Huysmans £7.99
Monsieur de Phocas – Jean Lorrain £8.99
Abbé Jules – Octave Mirbeau £8.99
Le Calvaire – Octave Mirbeau £7.99
The Diary of a Chambermaid – Octave Mirbeau £7.99
Torture Garden – Octave Mirbeau £7.99
Smarra & Trilby – Charles Nodier £6.99
Tales from the Saragossa Manuscript – Jan Potocki £5.99
Monsieur Venus – Rachilde £6.99
The Marquise de Sade – Rachilde £8.99
The Mysteries of Paris – Eugene Sue £6.99
The Wandering Jew – Eugene Sue £9.99
Micromegas – Voltaire £4.95

Forthcoming titles include:

The Dedalus Book of French Horror – edited by Terry Hale £8.99
Les Immensités – Sylvie Germain £8.99
L'Eclat du Sel – Sylvie Germain £8.99
The Enigma – Rezvani £8.99
L'Anglais décrit dans le château fermé – Pieyre de Mandiargues £8.99

Anthologies featuring French Literature in translation:

The Dedalus Book of Decadence – ed Brian Stableford £7.99
The Second Dedalus Book of Decadence – ed Brian Stableford £8.99
The Dedalus Book of Surrealism – ed Michael Richardson £8.99
Myth of the World: Surrealism 2 – ed Michael Richardson £8.99
The Dedalus Book of Medieval Literature – ed Brian Murdoch £8.99
The Dedalus Book of Femmes Fatales – ed Brian Stableford £8.99
The Dedalus Book of Sexual Ambiguity – ed Emma Wilson £8.99
The Decadent Cookbook – Medlar Lucan & Durian Gray £8.99
The Decadent Gardener – Medlar Lucan & Durian Gray £8.99

THE SQUARE

You have to lose your way seven times in the earth's labyrinth to be familiar with the echo, guardian of metals and stones, residing in its vaults; the greenish mask haunting its depths; the melancholy of its damp caves, refuge of secret thoughts and monsters. To a survivor of these strange regions the earth's surface appears covered with suckers, new snares to be overcome. Made fertile, the earth, once so light, grows heavy, a gigantic egg weighing on our feet like the eagle's prey in its claws.

Never before had I come to this neighbourhood. A scruffy rabble thronged the pavements, while a whole horde of grubby kids chased after each other down the street. At the number I was looking for, a great many address plates of all types and sizes gave the tenants' names and what floor they were on. At last, on a square of weather-yellowed paper, I read: A. FOHAT, OPHTHALMOLOGIST, 4th Floor. As I went through the gateway a fat woman, dressed in an old-fashioned jacket, appeared out of the dank shadows and stared at me. Without paying any attention to this apparition, I climbed the grimy steps of a staircase on the far side of the courtyard. At every stairhead, false doorways painted on to the damp walls gave a misleading impression of another floor, and I soon had go back down again to count more carefully the landings with real doors opening off them. It was with some effort that I got to the fourth floor. A large name-plate, which looked as if it had been put there only the day before, read ALEX-ANDRE FOHAT. The thickness of the walls prevented the noises from the street from reaching this far. I tugged violently on the bell-pull, so violently that it remained in my hand, while a whistling coil of wire lashed across my face. Quite aggrieved, I created such a rumpus that the tenants on the other floors, brought to their doors, soon raised a chorus of imprecation. In an extremely bad mood, I resigned myself to sitting on a step until silence returned. A smell of burnt fat mingled with that of cat's piss rising from the courtyard. What was I doing there on that staircase, cursing myself, with the darkness gathering in? A vague torpor must have overcome me; perhaps I even dozed. The building had long since fallen quiet again when a faint sound, close by, made me look round. The door was now wide open and standing in front of the doorway was a tall man, wrapped up, as if cold, in a long dressing gown. His brow was framed by two tiny flaps of white hair softly ruffled by the draught from the stairwell. The fellow had a thick scarf wound several times round his neck – and this was the month of July! But in this house, with decaying walls, that seemed truly outside of time, it could be that any sense of the seasons would eventually be lost.

'Monsieur Fohat, no doubt?' I said, getting to my feet.

The man gave an affirmative nod and stepped aside to let me in. Already I had forgotten the wait and all the little vexations I had suffered beforehand.

The first words the old man uttered threw me into bewilderment.

'Marcel Adrien, take a seat.'

How the devil did he know my name? At my astonishment, his normal expression, which seemed to be a perpetual smile, became more marked to the point of transforming itself into a grimace.

'Yes, I have a lot of information about you, as

indeed I do about all my clients. This is absolutely essential to my job, which does not, as you might think, consist of polishing and adjusting spectacles. All my present clients, and even future ones, have a file on their case in these drawers.'

As he said this, he pointed to a large number of drawers fitted into the four walls. Then the old man – but at that moment I forgot his aged appearance so youthful did his voice sound – leant forward to whisper in my ear (which I found rather disagreeable).

'I am thoroughly acquainted with your case.'

Then without attending to me any further, he began to put away the tortoiseshell frames scattered in front of him. Finally he went and sat at the other side of the now cleared table.

'Marcel Adrien,' he abruptly resumed, 'your case is not as unusual as you are tempted to believe. Myopia is a fairly common disorder . . .'

As a matter of fact, it was quite true that I had come to have my eyes tested – they had been giving me trouble for some time. Strange that it should have taken that word 'myopia' to remind me.

'. . . a fairly common disorder,' continued my interlocutor, 'in young people of your age. You suffer from a stricture of the optic organ. The abundance and diversity of the outside world, crowding at the entrance to this visual duct, causes distortion to the extremely fragile walls of the eyeball, which is liable to worsen.'

Having said this, the ophthalmologist stood up and went into the adjoining room. I felt a kind of relief at his departure. I do not know what had made me feel uneasy. After a few minutes in which I tried vainly to collect myself, Alexandre Fohat reappeared, bearing a large package, which he set down in front of me. And I heard him say to me in the tone of a doctor with other patients waiting, and in a faint voice, as though suddenly incomprehensibly far away:

'The treatment I prescribe for you is very simple; it merely requires a lot of patience and resolution. Follow the instructions to the letter and I promise you a sure improvement in your visual perceptions. Ah, I was forgetting!' he added in a voice that sounded close again, 'if in the meantime problems with your sight become more frequent, wear for an hour or two these spectacles that have been specially made up for you.'

So saying, he opened a drawer that he immediately slammed shut again, while his face became covered in confusion. I had time to glimpse several new dolls lined up in their boxes and I was about to give this shame-faced grandfather a knowing and indulgent smile. But the gravity, the severity of the gaze the ophthalmologist rested on me at that instant prevented me from doing so. Anyway, he immediately opened another drawer, and from a multitude of spectacle cases picked out one at random which he held out to me.

I found myself outside again quite shaken by this meeting. Dr Fohat's words were like a tangled skein whose thread eluded me. I walked down several

streets with the inward-turned gaze of one restoring
order to his thoughts. What did it matter to me now
which way I had come! Unconsciously, as I walked, I
pushed aside the gangs of children blocking the
entire width of the pavement. A woman I un-
intentionally jostled responded with a rude remark,
and I saw several laughing faces, among a group of
young people, turn to look at me. I must have borne
on my forehead evidence of my anxiety, and no
doubt it distorted my features in some comic way, for
I heard passers-by burst out laughing behind me and
saw the faces of those coming towards me broaden
into grins. But all this took place at some remove;
I registered it internally with nothing but indifference.

As I went on, another preoccupation came to the
fore: my package was beginning to intrigue people. A
man in a porter's uniform, such as one sees at railway
stations, even made so bold as to seize it from me. I
grabbed it back with a violent gesture. You did not
have to be a genius to see that the fellow was not a
real porter, that he had assumed this disguise only
the more easily to lay his hands on my property!
Running and staggering, I crossed avenues, bou-
levards, and bridges, I skirted endless building sites. I
must have covered a lot of ground, and yet it was
always as if I had just that moment emerged from
the ophthalmologist's. I walked, aimlessly now, down
long main streets thronged with a mass of workers
leaving their factories. While they swung their arms,
empty-handed, there was I, with my ridiculous
package, at once the focus of their attention. They

defiantly came right up to me, staring curiously as if intending to steal my thoughts as well as the contents of my parcel.

At last, having wandered in a maze of little streets and blind alleys, I came to a small square teeming with people of every description. Getting through a mob like that seemed beyond my strength, especially as the parcel was beginning to feel very heavy. Just then, I looked up and saw a sign: FURNISHED ROOM TO LET. I went down a narrow corridor at the end of which was a second sign that read: FOR ROOM TO LET, REFER TO OFFICE ON 1ST FLOOR. Now, this is a house to my liking, I said to myself. Here, at least, there's no lack of signs. No risk of getting lost, like at old Fohat's place or, as I just did, in this wretched neighbourhood.

On the first floor a woman of about thirty opened a glass-panelled door hung with pretty pink curtains. This woman gave me a key.

'It's the only room we have left. It's a bit small, but for a man on his own . . .'

She said these words as though she intended to convey something completely different, but I could not work out what she meant. Without torturing myself over a matter of such little importance, I took the key and climbed up several floors. All of a sudden the same woman appeared before me. How did she manage to get ahead of me? Was she so nimble that she slipped between my legs without my noticing? In any case I was surprised to see her there.

'This is it,' she said, letting me in.

16

It was indeed rather small: just room enough to get between the bed and the basin!

'I hope there's a window?' I grumbled, feeling rather cross.

'Oh, yes, monsieur, a real window!' replied the woman with a kind of sudden fervour.

And already the drawn curtain, flung-back shutters and open casements revealed to me, just a few feet away, a wall with an enormous window in it, surrounded by roof tops, chimney stacks and guttering.

'Wonderful view!' I added even more nastily.

'Oh, monsieur will get used to it!'

And without offering the slightest explanation of what connection there might be between these two statements, she went on: 'Look, that's my room, over there, almost opposite yours . . . '

I leant out, and was about to reply when I saw the window she had pointed to open and my soubrette, or landlady, appear at it, giving me a friendly wave. I was so astounded that I turned round, thinking it was a question of extraordinary resemblance. But no, she had disappeared. What sprightliness! I responded with a rather circumspect smile and closed both door and window of my new abode. Hardly had I bent over to cut the string round the parcel when I heard someone knocking, behind me. It was that woman again, literally moving with the speed of light. Would she spend the rest of her life shuttling between the two rooms? I was beginning to wonder with some anxiety. Examining her face more closely, I saw that she wore two superimposed masks of sadness and joy. Fitting badly over the former, which was older and more deeply embedded in her flesh – to the point where it looked as if it had been moulded on her features – the latter threatened to fall off at any moment. She said she had forgotten to tell me that she had fixed me up with a lampshade which would allow me to read in bed for as long as I wanted, without the owner of the building noticing. This thoughtfulness went straight to my heart. But unfortunately this kindly individual added, 'By casting the light directly on to the pages of your book, the lampshade will also save your eyesight . . .'

At the mention of my eyesight I felt perturbed. Was she aware of my infirmity? I was going to ask, but the expression on her face as I looked at her was so full of candour, emotional understanding, acceptance, and forgiveness of anything I might do or say, I at once came to the conclusion my question was pointless.

The parcel that had cost me so much effort to bring with me contained twenty cardboard boxes. To each one was attached a label with instructions that read: 'One pill to be taken daily on an empty stomach after twelve hours' work.'

'The old man's making fun of me,' I thought to myself. 'This is a stomach regimen.'

I opened one of the boxes. It was full of little blackish pills. It would take me a number of years to complete the treatment . . . Nevertheless, I resolved to begin the very next day. Finding work was, for me, not only a prerequisite of my recovery but also a dire necessity, for I had now completely run out of funds:

my remaining thirty-three francs would not even be enough to pay for the room. I then opened the spectacle case the ophthalmologist had given me. It contained a pair of spectacles that looked like the kind of sun-glasses you can buy anywhere, except that the lenses were so dark you could not see through them. I tried them on and was immediately plunged into total blackness. Groping my way, I lay down on the bed and soon fell asleep, without having had any supper.

When I woke up, at first I thought it was not yet light, then I felt the glasses still on the bridge of my nose! Removing them, I saw that the sunlight had long since reached into the furthest corners of my room, which, despite its crampedness, seemed less squalid than on the previous day. I opened the window. Leaning out of her window, smiling and bare-armed, was my landlady, waiting for me to appear in order to greet me with a fulsome 'Good morning, Monsieur Adrien!', as if we were old acquaintances.

'Good morning, good morning . . .' I said airily.

Through the huge glass window blocking my horizon, I saw workers in grey overalls engaged in packing. Others were at their tasks and I was still idling! I quickly went downstairs. My neighbour – she had had time to change and get down to her office – came and stood outside her door when she heard my footsteps.

'Did you sleep well, Monsieur Adrien?'

I gave her to understand that I was in a terrible hurry and rushed off, not without having noticed that the ROOM TO LET sign had disappeared. The square was not so busy as the day before, although a good many people were already out and about, their paths crossing, or overtaking each other, some in haste, others just standing there, cloud-gazing. I did not know what direction to take, but so as not to appear hesitant in the event that my landlady might have been observing me from her window, I almost ran across the road and entered the first shop I came to.

'I've come about the job vacancy ...' I hazarded.

I was handed a grey overall, and I immediately set to work.

Dr Fohat's treatment did not specify what kind of work should precede the swallowing of each tablet. Abhorring all manner of specialization, and not being aware of having any particular aptitude, I was prepared to do anything in the way of life's little chores, such as sawing wood, brushing clothes, fixing handles into brooms, etc. The main thing, for my regimen to bear fruit, was the duration of these tasks. 'One pill to be taken daily on an empty stomach after twelve hours' work' – those were the doctor's orders. In this excellent frame of mind, I began my day as general handyman at Andco & Co. I have always felt sorry for those compelled by their jobs to go through the same motions every day, without the slightest room for imagination. The happy diversity of duties assigned to me in that respectable establishment, with no other recommendation but my appearance, so suited my temperament that I went on working till evening without a break. At such willingness, my head of department summoned me to his office at the end of that very first day to inform me of the decision of the managing director of Andco & Co. to increase by one-third the salary he had originally intended to award me. Having no other ambition but to secure the prompt recovery of my visual faculties, I did not much care about this favourable outcome. When I found myself back on the street that evening, I had not eaten anything since the day before and I was beginning to suffer violent stomach cramps. But I was very pleased with myself. I had difficulty getting through the crush in the square. The landlady was in the corridor, watching out for me. Like a grateful wife or young mistress throwing off all restraint after being kept waiting, she threw her arms round my neck, and in response to this impulsive demonstration of warmth I had no option but to hug her tightly in my arms before climbing up to my room.

I would not have put my faith in the ophthalmologist's treatment for any length of time, had it not given me some immediate evidence of its efficacy. The reader will remember what relief the spectacles afforded me by plunging me into a salutary slumber. Now, no sooner had I swallowed the first pill than my stomach-ache ceased. Shrewd minds will perhaps think that this power to suppress hunger has nothing to do with the alleviation of visual disturbances. Yet, only the one who is supposed to cure us knows what we need. I suspected that this miracle was what the person who had pondered, calculated and assessed the

effects of my regimen had intended, and I took the
decision to go without any form of nourishment from
then on other than the consumption of my tablets. It
would mean a considerable saving to my purse. The
thought of this reminded me I had not yet discussed
the price of my room. As I made my way to the landlady's office to settle this matter, I wondered what
approach to adopt after that moment of excessive
familiarity between us the night before. The door
with the pretty pleated curtains was standing ajar.
Through the opening I glimpsed the young woman,
looking worried, and deeply involved in examining
herself in the mirror. But at my arrival the engaging
smile she always had for me reappeared on her face.
When I told her the purpose of my visit, she came up
close to me to explain, with languor in her voice and,
occasionally, in such passionate tones I had difficulty
in correctly interpreting her words, that she was not
the owner of this establishment but, like me, just a
tenant. Not knowing how to pass her time, she spent
it working for the guest-house, a job that was no great
burden to her for the very good reason there was only
one room to let, which was precisely the one I had just
moved into. So all her spare time would now be her
own. As for the price of the room in question, this was
of no importance: when the owner came by, she would
ask. She added that her name was Edith. All of this
conversation, in which I detected some embarrass-
ment on her part, brought a surprising animation to
her face. Warmer blood now coloured her features,
dispelling the faint lines. When she told me her name,
she suddenly became very beautiful.

It was so dark when I tried to return to my pad that I ended up in the wrong room – or perhaps my bad eyesight was the sole cause of this mistake? In the room I went into, I could not distinguish very much at first, but as my eyes grew accustomed to the gloom they were soon able to pick out from their setting the people moving about in it. They were two old crocks, so covered with wrinkles I could not tell how old they were. However great the number of years that came to mind, I had only to look at them to see how far short of the mark I was in my estimation. They were certainly over a hundred. Their brows had the spongy look of decaying walls, and their mouths were like the cracked curbs of old wells. In the midst of this decrepitude, only their pale eyes still flickered, like faded lamps. I was about to retreat, apologizing for having intruded on their privacy, when the woman, clinging to my arm with astonishing strength, begged me to stay, if only for just a moment, to make each other's acquaintance. But I was no sooner settled in one of the lace-covered armchairs than the wheedling old crone had already forgotten me. I took advantage of this to observe the goings-on of these two contemporaries of a bygone human race.

On my arrival the man had slipped under the eiderdown on a double bed and, all the time the old woman was extending her courtesies to me, he moaned quietly, as though annoyed no one was paying attention to him any more. Now his big contented head was nodding on the pillow while she gazed at him affectionately, tucking him up and making a fuss of him. Nor did the spectacle end there! The two dotards began to caress each other, in a parody of youthful gestures horrible to behold. Oh! the tremblings of their skeletal hands! In their toothless mouths words that in young people are excused by the delirium of passion sounded blasphemous. At last, tearing herself away from this debauchery, the old woman went over to a dresser adorned with two glass domes under which some unspeakable scraps were mouldering away. She brought out a saucer containing some little sugar-cubes, then, recalling my presence, with an appalling grimace no doubt intended to express tenderness she murmured, 'Yes, sir, he can't go to sleep without his little sugar-cubes . . . Can you, my big bow-wow?'

The old man nodded, as he did to all of his companion's actions. I had seen more than my patience could bear. It was a relief to return to the solitude of my cell on the floor below, its bareness looking comfortable in comparison with the clutter of junk I had just left. A blur danced before my eyes and I did not waste much time in putting on Dr Fohat's spectacles.

What was it that the workers behind the big glass window were so busy at? For the first few days I thought it was packing, and I would not have given the matter any further thought had I not noticed, on opening my window one morning, the abnormal haste with which these men and women would conceal the objects they were handling, or rush to draw the curtain, hiding themselves from my view. There was no doubt they did not like the feeling of being observed by someone emerging from sleep. I asked Edith how she explained this attitude and what mysterious task these people could possibly be engaged in. But as soon as she realized what I was talking about, she became profoundly sad: until then, she had thought the first thing I looked for every morning was her. Yet it was not my fault if this glass window lay directly in my line of vision, whereas Edith's window, although much closer, was a little to one side. I consoled her as best I could. Was she not attaching too much importance to mere trifles? The fact that I was intrigued by what was happening behind a glass window detracted nothing from the pleasure afforded by a charming neighbour's radiant early-morning smile and bare arms.

'You're right,' she finally admitted, 'but why concern yourself with those people? If you knew what goes on behind all these walls, you'd be absolutely amazed!'

I could see she immediately regretted having let slip these words, and I guessed she was the holder of a secret too onerous for her. I could also see that she would not tell me any more that day. So, in order to win her trust and explain that I did not want to be indebted to her, I recounted my error of the previous evening. She soon began to laugh, but this was to hide her confusion. Immediately I referred to the couple who were contemporaries of Methuselah, her cheeks flushed and she strove to hide from me the ardent passion smouldering in her eyes by averting her gaze.

I would have been extremely embarrassed to have

had to define my responsibilities at Andco & Co. I was allowed to combine the utmost freedom with the requirements of my job. I had no set time for any of my duties and could go from one to the other without incurring reproach. Having been entrusted with the cleaning of part of the premises, I could empty great buckets of water under the feet of employees in the middle of the day, or cover the offices with a thick layer of dust, and no one was entitled to object. If I felt like breaking off from my task, leaving brooms and feather dusters among the bookkeepers' accounts, I was equally free to do so. All that mattered was that the work should be done. Needless to say, nothing of the sort happened, and I tried hard not to get in anyone's way. There was just one chore that was more of a burden than the others. One of the directors had two enormous mastiffs I was responsible for feeding each day. For this, I had to go to the kitchens located in an annex on the other side of the square, right by my lodgings. I had to walk along the edge of a fairly long stretch of crowded pavement, in full view of everyone, with my two containers of greasy steaming liquid. This was not always achieved without detriment to the stockings of a female passer-by or the trousers of a male pedestrian. And my great fear was of meeting Edith while I was about it, or that she might see me one day from her window. Naturally she imagined I held a position at Andco & Co. very different from that of swill-carrier. Ah! if she had only known what I did not mind handling, regardless of how degrading – quite the contrary – from the brush for scrubbing the lavatories, to the silk-bristled clothes' brush reserved for the chief clerk's dress coat. And that is only to mention objects! But I accepted, I sought out without fastidiousness the most unsavoury tasks. Not from any dubious desire for humiliation, but solely from fear of performing with joy what ought to have been effort and toil for me. According to the prescriptions of my regimen, these twelve hours had to be twelve hours of work, and not some enjoyable or interesting pastime. It was not in Edith's nature to understand these reasons. So I preferred to keep her in the dark about my pursuits that were too much at odds with those of the specialist engineer, or academic lawyer, or of any other occupation requiring some refinement, or love.

Andco & Co. employed a large staff. Seeing the shop, with its two narrow windows looking out on the square, no one would never have suspected the amount of business done by this firm. What kind of business? It was as difficult to know this as it was to say how many were employed in it. Above me were too many hierarchically organized, interdependent departments for a humble employee of the lowest rank, like myself, to be able to penetrate this complexity. Perhaps I might have been able to find out something from the underlings around me, all of them older than myself, but since learning of my 'excessive zeal', they did not look on me kindly. Besides, the particular job that I had kept me permanently isolated from the feelings among the staff. I was not part of the works there. I may say, I was not even the grease that oiled those works, hardly even the canister containing the oil. To what absurdity does the pursuit of an image lead: here I am, reduced to the shadow of an oil-can! Such a nonentity, after being once snubbed, did not venture again to ask any questions.

My colleagues could not accept that I should put in twelve hours' work a day, on my own initiative, when they were trying so devilishly hard to trim a few minutes off the length of their shifts. Privately I had to admit they had good reason, so grim did their lives seem, so dead-end and hopeless, when I myself was sustained by the thought of recovery! It was this that prompted me to accept and seek out the lowliest of tasks. But I could no more get them to understand than I could Edith, that these tasks had been prescribed for me, that I was here undergoing treatment, for reasons of health. To have admitted this would have provoked laughter in these people who were so confident of their good eyesight it gave them cause for arrogance. They could not tell by looking at me that I was ill. But anyway, what did their ignorance and lack of understanding matter! Despite the sniggers and sly scheming my behaviour was going to incur, I had to keep my eyes fixed on my objective: that of gaining a clear perception of things.

My day-to-day existence continued to be organized on a temporary basis. Yet, faced with the many boxes still full of tablets, I felt crushed by the certainty that this temporariness would extend for more than a good part of my life, and perhaps my entire life. I dared not even calculate the time needed for my cure. Maybe I should not have set my sights so high, and thought only, for example, of curing my chilblains or toothaches, rather than such an essential organ as the eye. Unquestionably, remedying these lesser ailments would not have taken years. Perhaps I should have thought only of earning my living, like everyone else, without even bothering about my more or less imaginary little infirmities. Now, there was a simple, clearly defined goal! Only my pride deemed it too easy. Too easy, yes, too easy for me, now that I had no expenses, no needs, and could save my entire salary almost without thinking about it. But before consenting to the immediate advantages the treatment had brought me, would I not have done better to accept, like everyone else, this simple, clearly defined goal? For those who had to find the money to feed themselves every day, it was not such an easy goal.

Once I was embarked on this regimen, devoted to following the instructions to the letter, I came to lose all notion of reality. To reverse matters, I would have had to leave Edith, Andco & Co., and the square, to break all these ties and return to where I came from, to my point of departure, to go back to Dr Fohat's and tell him, 'I've changed my mind. It's not my eyesight that's giving me problems, it's my hearing, or my hair. Yes, my dear Dr Fohat, can you imagine, my hair aches . . .'

No, I could see that would not do.

'My toes ache . . . There's nothing wrong with me at all any more, I want to live like other people, like everyone else, I want my old problems back again, in order to overcome them by myself and not to have to overcome the ones you've suggested to me . . .'

No, that would not do. I would get tangled up in woolly explanations. And I could almost see the ophthalmologist now, walking over to his drawers and pulling out my file, while I remained crushed by the evidence – the evidence of my visual disorders, the evidence of their necessary cure, the evidence of my destiny. No, I could not go back now. I had to come to terms with this temporary existence, even if it were to last for ever – especially if it were to last for ever.

The neighbourhood where I had ended up was surely the most wretched slum-heap imaginable. Immediately on being wrested from sleep, all that the populace inhabiting these hovels was anxious to do was get some fresh air. So, from the crack of dawn, the scene in the streets around the square was akin both to a gypsy camp and a leper colony. From the seedy lanes and alleyways rose smells that would put to flight an army of sewer-men. Squalor, a triumphant squalor, overlay people and things. Through the open doorways of certain bars, scabby old men applied themselves to scratching their wounds while at the bar counter sipping at a drink that looked like urine. Alongside them, whores, with sticky lips and faces plastered with greasepaint, yawned as they pulled up the grimy shoulder-straps of their blouses. Some big fat women – mobile barrels that looked as if they had two of those sacks that serve as ballast for balloonists attached to them – lolled about on the pavements, engaged in the task of grinding a 'coffee' consisting largely of grains of barley that a gang of urchins, down on all fours, picked out of the horse-dung.

For the first few days my poor eyesight shielded me from these details and a great many others that were the manifestation of the most abject poverty. When I became aware of this pestilential environment, my first instinct was to rush back every evening to my tiny room, a veritable haven of grace. I have to say that the small square where I lived, the centre of this vast Court of Miracles, was as though miraculously preserved from the surrounding contagion. Its facades, trompe-l'oeil constructions fronting tumbledown shacks, were deluding. You reached this oasis via the three main roads without suspecting the labyrinth of ruts and blind alleys encircling it. A salubrious impression of a decent working-class district prevailed. As long as you did not leave the area, life was possible among these twenty or so disparate shops imbued on occasion with the charm of old provincial squares. Alas! behind this facade lay not the infinite tranquillity of the countryside but a fetid swamp of every vice and crime. I wondered how Edith could possibly have grown used to this neighbourhood. It is true that, restricting her life to the comings and goings in the square, she seemed unaware of the sordid zone around it. This indifference was not peculiar to her; all the inhabitants of the square likewise avoided the oppressive blight on the periphery. Where they lived, there was no evidence, or almost none, of the ugliness and squalor lurking only twenty yards away. It was only my 'insane curiosity', as Edith so rightly put it, that made me so quickly aware of these appalling environs. This did not make me any more proud of myself. Is it possible to camp on the edge of an abyss without having the curiosity to peer into it? Even if everyone else around me managed to get on with the business of living their lives without worrying about the ever present danger of the shifting sands near by, I could not resign myself to such wisdom, to such blindness. I was drawn to this open quagmire, so close by. And soon I began to venture back there again, certainly not with enjoyment, but perhaps with a kind of perverse pleasure, as if in the buried hope of finding there, once my pity was exhausted, several other reasons for persisting in my course.

I still suffered terribly, although less frequently, from my eye problems, and I was overwhelmed one evening with momentary despair. I felt tempted once more to give up Dr Fohat's treatment. There must be another, more rapid treatment, to be found if I looked for it. But at that moment Edith – it could only have been her – knocked at my door. I hastily slipped the box of tablets under the bolster and, as soon as she came in, to hide my confusion I vehemently asked whether or not she had found out the price of the room.

'I absolutely insist on paying for my lodgings . . . I'm in no need whatsoever of free accommodation' – and so on.

My almost rude insistence plunged her into a despondency that took me by surprise. All her vivaciousness suddenly drained away. Fearing I had been too brutal, I took her by the hands and consoled her without knowing exactly what had upset her.

'Why do you only want to make me unhappy,' she said through her tears.

At last, after a long while, she consented to tell me that she had seen the owner of the guest-house that very morning in fact, but the price of the room had not been discussed, even though they had talked non-stop about me.

When I expressed my surprise and disappointment, she murmured, 'Well, I can see I'm going to have to tell you the whole story . . .'

I had suspected from the start this was no ordinary guest-house. But how could I have imagined that living under this roof I would become the victim of downright blackmail? As she recounted the following details, Edith all the while protested her good faith and innocence. But the more I thought about it, the more I told myself that, even as she protested in this way, she never for a moment stopped playing her part. No, this was no ordinary guest-house. I had on several occasions had the peculiar impression of being the sole lodger, so oppressive was the silence of the staircases and corridors. There was only Edith's winged footstep, on her way upstairs every evening, a few minutes after me, to disturb the heavy stillness. I knew that she then watched me from her window, a discreet and zealous spy. Apart from this little game, no sign of life attested to any human presence in the building. After my encounter with the two old crocks, I happened to open the door of yet another room by mistake – once again, because of my poor eyesight. In the same gloom, I glimpsed another two old crocks, just as horrible as the first and just as affectionately paired, wrapped in each other's arms, snuggled up in an identical armchair, in front of a row of yellowing photographs lined up on an old dresser. I quickly fled at the sight of these other two amorous mummies. Was this house an old people's home?

Edith's long story both confirmed and invalidated my assumptions. The building had once housed a doll factory. On the death of the owner, it became the property of his great-niece. Being a philanthropic soul, the young lady resolved to transform these unneeded workshops into a moderately priced boarding-house where the poor would find shelter. Having put up a ROOMS TO LET sign outside, she waited, full of confidence in her good intentions. However, her plans were overturned by the first client to show up. He was a young man who had strayed into the neighbourhood owing to circumstances totally beyond his control. Being a person of simple tastes, he rented the top-floor room ('the one you're living in now, Monsieur Adrien', Edith murmured, a marked solemnity distinguishing these words from the rest of her account). This first lodger, having seen the owner of the building at the window opposite his own that very evening, took such a fancy to her that he asked her to marry him. The two young people were very happy and the young woman realized her mistake: what the majority of people were most in want of was not housing but love. As this enterprising person could not run a business that in any way ran counter to her deepest held convictions, she immediately resolved to change the purpose of the guest-house to conform with her ideal. If two people had found happiness in so relatively uncomplicated a manner, there was no doubt that with the necessary refinement this procedure could work again. A young girl, preferably poor and with the desire to marry, would be taken on as manageress. Her sole task would be to let the upstairs room to the first male client to present himself, and then to appear before him at every opportunity. The lower floors would be reserved for the multiple couples bound to result from this ingenious scheme.

So, many years went by, to the greatest good of those who came to seek refuge in the guest-house. The perfect organization of this peculiar kind of marriage bureau seemed to escape the law whereby everything bears within it the seed of its own destruction. The miraculous 'strokes of luck', allowing so many couples to discover the meaningfulness of their lives, kept recurring with infallible regularity. When the rooms below were no longer sufficient to accommodate the 'product', as it were, of the rooms above, the founder's proverbial benevolence was put to the test. But once again this honourable person – she was by now an old lady – found a solution to the problem: from then on, only the oldest couples were to live in the building. All the others, and their families as they came along, would be asked to leave, to fend for themselves elsewhere.

It was then, from the time when this measure

of expediency stopped the inevitable overcrowding, that an interesting phenomenon occurred: that spark of engagement between the two attic rooms became much less frequent. Sometimes a number of tenants succeeded each other before one was caught in the nets laid for him. Were these defections to be attributed to the fear of tomorrow, or quite simply to the fact that the initial atmosphere was slightly chilled by the presence of so many old folk in the building? No one ever knew. But the owner, now an imposing matron, thought it best to make one last decision before her retirement: the inhabitants of the lower rooms were absolutely forbidden to show their faces outside their lodgings. And the guest-house continued, willy-nilly, to tack across the dark-light sea of its destiny, without any further change occurring to modify its progress.

While confessing these circumstances to me, Edith's face had the calmness of shutters about to burst open. She talked so volubly that her lips remained still despite the constant flow of words issuing from them. Clearly, even though she regretted having to reveal these facts, it was a relief to her to confide in me. But it was only to replace the old burden with a new one. When she had to confess her role and position in this strange household, I saw her anxiety, how she hung on my gaze: knowing what the set-up is, will he now break out of this Machiavellian imbroglio?

'When I came to work in the guest-house,' she went on humbly, 'I didn't have the necessary dedication to submit to its regulations. That's probably why things went wrong: my aspirations, not being completely directed towards the purpose of this organization, my aspirations failed to honour its rules. A first tenant took this room. But at that time I spent my evenings reading and I must have given him the impression, from behind my window-panes, of being an old church hen buried in her missal. A second tenant turned up. Instead of laughing with him and showing myself off in front of him, as the regulations laid down, I overwhelmed him with questions (and answers, alas!) about philosophy and metaphysics. After showing interest for the first few days, he quickly tired of my foolish pretensions. A third one came, and then a fourth. I put them all off, with my seriousness, my incompetence in making the most of my attractions, or my indifference.

'What senseless pride prompted me to resist when I should have submitted, to reject when I should have taken? I was twenty, and despised this inveiglement, this wrongful deed that all women of my age had been conniving with each other for centuries to achieve. I was just a link in the chain, and now, because of me, the chain was in danger of being broken. By not accepting my role, how many others was I preventing from playing theirs with a sincerity I was incapable of?

'Wanting to mend my ways, I fell into the trap of going to the opposite extreme. I was so eager to put in an appearance, so bold in my smiles, so suggestive in my remarks that my successive guests saw my advances as nothing but cheap flirtatiousness and immediately rebuffed me. By the time I realized my new mistake, the years had passed. I was no longer young. The next man to come along would be my last chance. One morning, with the last trembling hope of desperation, I hung a ROOM TO LET sign over the door. It was you who came that day.'

The confusion and welter of contradictory feelings into which Edith's account plunged me prevented me from immediately taking a decision that would have saved me from this fly-trap. Nothing would induce me to enter into these ready-made plans for a happiness I did not aspire to. It was imperative, above all, to remain a free agent, and not get so much as the tip of my little finger involved in these complications. That is what I wanted to convey to my friend. However, with her usual adroitness, she did not wait to discover the outcome of my reflections, but slipped away, no more enlightened than before, and preferring not to be rather than learn of an irrevocable decision on my part.

I would have to look for another hotel. But in the days that followed, I discovered that, short of accepting some vile flea-infested hovel above a rowdy bar, there was no sign for kilometres around of even the most modest lodgings. As for moving away and finding work elsewhere, changing my life in short, this required more energy than I now had. I contented myself with slipping under the door of the office an envelope containing a reasonable sum for the rental of my room. I felt that by seeing to it that my accommodation was no longer free of charge, I would be releasing myself from any other obligation.

But that very same evening I found the money lying on my table. At that moment, I was struck for the first time by the uselessness of this sterile wealth I was secreting like a poison and which was accumulating, outside of me, every week. Soon I would be like the possessor of a fortune in a country where this money was not legal tender.

As darkness fell over the rooftops, hiding the big glass window from my gaze (a double curtain had been hung over it, from the inside, but I could tell from various indications that the mysterious activity continued behind it), I imagined myself, up at my narrow window, the lone pilot of a large steamer specializing in honeymoon trips. Inside the hull of my ship, one hundred amorous couples embraced each other in silence, while I, with my hand on the tiller, kept safe their naive delusion from the reef they could not see. Then, at the recollection of those dreadful old folk, I cursed aloud the fate that made me the guardian of these dead who were still pretending to be alive.

Edith appeared at her dormer window, and I immediately slammed shut the casements of mine, as I might have stepped on her face and turned away without looking to see if her grimace was one of resentment or suffering. Hastily grabbing my spectacles, I fell into a deep sleep.

Speaking of my spectacles, I must say that for quite a while I had been noticing some very strange things about using them. Whereas in the evening they would dispel my tiredness and always help me to sleep, during the day they were of no aid at all any more. In vain would I feverishly don them; not only did things continue to dance in front of me but it seemed, through those opaque lenses, that people around me were bursting into laughter. In short, more than being of any use, these dark glasses were making me looking ridiculous. Every evening now, before putting them on, I took care to close my window, for fear that Edith might see them and laugh at me. Even the relief I would then get from them was far from being as complete as at the beginning of the treatment. And I was beginning to wonder if the sleep they afforded me was not due quite simply to the total darkness or a kind of auto-suggestion. I was beginning to suspect Dr Fohat of having made a fool of me, at least with regard to these glasses, and to have only included them in the treatment so as not to rob me of an illusion – the illusion that it is precisely the job of an ophthalmologist to provide spectacles.

Edith had for a while put me back in touch with reality. But since her confession we were determined to avoid each other, she so that she could continue to live without knowing what I had decided, and I to avoid getting myself any more deeply ensnared in the trap she had revealed to me. The work-and-sleep rhythm imposed by Dr Fohat's treatment was now interrupted only by my day off. To tell the truth, I felt no need at all of this rest. But since there was no mention in the instructions of a weekly break being detrimental to the treatment, I took advantage of that day off to afford myself a little taste of other people's lives.

I was less and less loathe to venture into the teeming streets close to the square. These excursions were a kind of defiance of Edith and her stay-at-home entourage, and of the people of the square, too. They would not have wandered, as I did, down those winding streets crowded with the most sickening specimens of humanity: slovenly tarts, yobs in dirty caps with a cigarette-end behind one ear, cafe waiters with insolent gazes, shop assistants dressed up in their Sunday best, their cheeks pitted by smallpox. An intense pity sometimes overcame me in the face of these human dregs that reflected incurable poverty. Here was I, complacently following my treatment to improve my eyesight, when all these people around me were blind! Should I not have been bathing their gummy eyelids with buckets full of water, scrubbing their filthiness, exposing their suppurating wounds, before worrying about my own eyesight, which, after all, was not that bad! Yes, truly, I would feel full of remorse. I also tried to comprehend such inequality.

One day a child of seven or eight, chased by a ragged screaming horde, came round a bend and threw herself into my arms. It seemed to me, at that moment, that her terror-filled face was not yet tainted with the depravities of her clan. But as she recognized in her saviour an inhabitant of the square, a boundless dread immediately drove from her eyes the trust shown by her initial gesture. When I saw her again the following week she gave me a bawdy look, and I failed to understand how I could for one minute have taken any interest in the girl, who was already ridden with vice just like all the others.

Around that time, I happened once again, on

returning to the hotel, to end up in the wrong room again. The two old crocks I discerned in the gloom were even more decrepit and shrivelled than the ones on the two previous occasions. Their faces were like rotten apples left in a barn. But never the less there was movement and a licking of lips. I noticed some jars, lined up in front of them on an old-fashioned chimney-piece, in which, I am sure, were mouldering foetuses.

Wandering through the stinking streets, I would sometimes see a creature appear, as though rising out of a hole in the ground, who no longer bore any human resemblance, such were the degradation and despair expressed in its features. Sometimes no trace even of despair was left on this mask, on which ignominy, avowed and accepted, took on the look of provocation. Everyone would move away, and all I could make out, from the murmurings that accompanied this wretch, was that it came from the square. Another time it was a child with its hands cut off, held out with upraised arms by its mother, screaming with horror. On yet other occasions a young girl would stagger down the street, sniggering in an idiot fashion and lifting her skirts. All of them, and so many others I am at a loss to describe, in among this bunch of pariahs, in this sordid zone that was a repository of every form of rottenness – all, I now knew, came from the square. I also knew they had once been creatures of innocence and purity, unsullied creatures. Since making their fateful move, away from the countryside and the fresh air where they lived then, to that seemingly respectable square, they had been stripped of everything. In the face of such injustices the absurdity of my own treatment and the scant importance of its results became more obvious to me. For I, who by luck had so far been saved from their abjection, knew these victims were not to blame. And I could not help shuddering at the thought that I rubbed shoulders every day with those guilty of so many crimes. Perhaps my indifference to everything but my cure favoured their perpetration.

Everything around me was so complicated and intertwined that my private life seemed linked with external things, seemed to be those external things. Evidently, there was incessant traffic between the square, miraculously preserved from poverty, and the surrounding area. But by what subterranean routes and secret alleys was this traffic conducted? I had to elucidate the mystery surrounding these subhumans, reflections of a dark world seething inside me. My first thought was to go and find Edith, to draw on her long experience of the square. Then I gave up that idea. Edith had spent too much time learning her part to know about anyone else's. Everything went on around her without making any impression on her. Did she not have enough with her own obsession: to confine me, with her, in one of the guest-house's family vaults!

My colleagues, though, could not be unaware of the clandestine traffic I had just discovered. By cross-checking, I might perhaps succeed in learning something from them. Despite my reluctance, I would have to overcome my isolation, my pride and theirs; I would have to coax them, win their confidence. But, even knowing in advance the danger such a tactic would entail, I was ready to sacrifice discretion, self-respect, and any semblance of dignity. To understand, our gaze must become a gaze of love, but that gaze at once gives rise to a compromise that nothing can cancel. Perhaps I was wrong in deliberately accepting this compromise, deliberately deviating towards this new goal. Everything around me brightened up, became differently enlivened. Till that day, I had been like a wall which people passed by. My humility transformed this wall into a mirror and others' souls were soon reflected in it. First of all I selected those of my colleagues whose attitudes and behaviour were most contrary to my lifestyle, those I despised the most. When I understood perfectly the differences between us, I tried to be like them by disregarding my personal preferences and adopting theirs. They quickly felt drawn to me, and I knew I had won their sympathy. I, the lowly sweeper, Mr Mop as I was often called, became the confidant of the most senior heads of department in Andco & Co.

One after the other, they revealed to me the seamy side of their jobs, their covert life. Many were unmitigated scoundrels, not to say perfect criminals. They belonged, as I did, to the most huge organization for blackmail, robbery and felony that anyone could conceive of – and all this, behind the respectable facade of a company that, despite the indeterminate nature of its activity, attracted no suspicion. Every member of staff, in addition to his official job (maintenance, book-keeping, etc.), was charged with a special mission to be fulfilled on the outside, as soon as night fell. No one knew what any-one else's mission consisted of, but everyone knew they were all guilty in this affair. And until that day I thought I was the only one with a secret life! I was shocked to discover such an abundance of concealed abysses behind the innocuous appearances of other people's lives.

An endless compromise, an endless lie, no purity whatsoever. Only, the fact that most of them, one day or another, would join the ranks of the victims cast an aura of pitifulness over their lives. But what did they know about it? Right up till the last minute they revelled, with such assurance, such imperturb-able confidence, among the ranks of the torturers! Their initial good intentions, their original inno-cence, all foundered eventually, no one knew where, no one knew why. Everyone was very proud of their mission: from the moment each of them was entrusted with it, nothing else counted any more! With what sombre impatience they would then await the end of the day to start stalking! For hunting was what it was all about, hunting of a keen and ruthless kind. The most difficult thing for the person charged with the mission was to keep up a good front, an expression that did not arouse suspicion about his intentions in advance. But darkness came to the aid of those who felt diffident about such deviousness. For a long time I wondered where these nocturnal operations, these outrages boasted of by their authors with such disconcerting equanimity, took place. I soon learned that once darkness had fallen the square itself could conceal numerous crimes. There were also deserted areas, with stagnating puddles and sinister reflections, at the end of nearby lanes, that at night were crawling with a regular mob of stalkers lying in wait; there were dead-end alleys that no one who had the misfortune to venture into them could return from entirely themselves. I shuddered to think that even yesterday I could have been so close to these places without being aware of them, without having any inkling of what they were used for.

All these revelations upset me so much that one evening I succumbed to the temptation to tell Edith about them. When she divined my intention of breaking the silence established between us, she thought her last hour had come, or at least such was the impression she gave me. But a kind of calm came over her when she realized from my very first words that I would not be talking about her or myself. Soon she was listening closely, almost devoutly. The twilight effaced the lines on her face. When she understood what was at issue – after a considerable while – a shudder ran through her and the deepest despondency came over her as I continued talking. I recalled how that same sadness had taken hold of her the day I questioned her about the glass window. The memory of this made me suspect that the two things were connected. And, as before, I guessed that Edith, although she had never made any reference to them in my presence, knew all about them. But her sadness disarmed me, and seeing that I was not revealing anything new to her, I abruptly fell silent rather than interrogate her.

We were both seated on the edge of my bed, staring at the rectangle of open sky before us. Above the invisible roof-tops, four solitary cables of a high-voltage electric power line underscored, all but imperceptibly, the half-light of dusk. And suddenly a night-bird settled on one of these cables. We clearly saw its grey wrinkled eyelids open several times and the strange luminous pupils gaze at us. Then this visitor flew off with a silky rustle. Edith's body weighed so little, next to mine, that I felt it involuntarily lean towards me, tipping into the hollow formed by my own weight on the bed, as if it were made of some extremely light substance, meringue or balsa wood. And yet I could tell it was alive, but it had the airy freedom of movement that pure spirits must have. All my thoughts were occupied by what I had learned in recent weeks at Andco & Co. But something eluded me: the connection between my indignation and this sudden silence, my room, Edith, this mysterious bird, myself.

I no longer wanted to know whether the obscurity slowly descending before my eyes were the evening shadows or simply a recurrence of my former ailment. This wilful ignorance, this refusal, this sudden spiritlessness made me very happy, although conscious of my lassitude. How simple it would be to remain there, not to go any further, simply to take between my hands the hands of this woman whose silent presence all at once had acquired a heavenly quality! But turning to look at her face, I saw a gleam of such hope appear in the depths of her eyes that I felt a sudden pang of oppressive anxiety. The hotel and its cargo of old folk resurfaced in my mind. I abruptly got to my feet to send Edith away. But she had already vanished from sight, like some unformulated, shadow of remorse, and in the darkness that had now finally descended I heard the shutters of her room close, creaking like a rusty shop-sign.

The real crime cannot be denying myself to Edith, safeguarding my independence at all costs. If there is, for me, any crime, or complicity in crime, which comes to the same thing, is it not rather in continuing to turn up every morning at Andco & Co. as if nothing were amiss? For I no longer have the excuse of not knowing. I now know what appalling skulduggery, what despicable vileness the business undertaken by this firm amounts to. Is the strength of my will so diminished that I cannot take the only decision the situation calls for: to leave this neighbourhood, quit my job, and go and live elsewhere, even if it means interrupting Dr Fohat's treatment for a while.

Of course I found good reasons for overcoming my scruples: my job differed in every respect from the sinister activities of my colleagues. Is he who polishes the shoes of an assassin every morning to be called an assassin? Is he who cleans the rooms of a gang of crooks every day to be called a thief? No, I felt in no way implicated in this affair. And yet the money for my salary is stolen money, the air I breathe all day long is fouled by the breath of shameless traffickers; my masters are villains and I know it. They have need of my services and I know it. Although not involved in their shady deals, I enrich myself by their profitable outcome. I do so even more surely and rapidly than the others, because of the extreme sobriety of my life! A contemptible receiver of stolen goods – that is what I am in reality. My hands regard themselves as innocent because they have never dared try out the weapon they polish every day. My heart regards itself as pure because it has never had the courage to give way to impurity. Actually, the least grain of dust here is guilty, and I who daily raise myriad grains of dust, on the specious pretext of removing it, am also guilty. Who knows whether, without my services, the others would agree to render theirs? Perhaps I am the only absolutely indispensable cog in this machine! And I cannot work hard enough, and because of my own personal health I continue to give twelve hours of my life every day so that all these crimes can be committed! Actually I am involved, I am guilty, just as guilty as the invisible and silent master who commands this army of brigands, albeit I am the humblest, most *visible* and most unruly of his servants. (In this peculiar factory, degree of importance seemed to be measured according to invisibility.) But the more deep-rooted my sense of responsibility became, and the more my 'good reasons' revealed themselves to be bad ones, the more I clung to my job.

On my day off the following Thursday, even though it was early I only managed to get across the square by worming my way through the crowd. The explanation for such a throng was no longer a mystery to me. While the unavowed dealings of the inhabitants of the square with those of the neighbouring streets took place at night and by routes so secret that no one was able to witness them, their official comings and goings occurred within closed confines and always went through the square. Hence, this continual to-and-fro within such small area of people going about their work or leisure. Yet the deserted look of the shops on such a lively square continued to surprise me. It is true that it had never entered my head to go into one of them. The rather unprepossessing appearance of the shop-fronts must have been the reason for this disregard. But that morning I had the feeling that by pushing open one of these doors, I would learn a little of all that remained unknown to me.

'How can I help you?' asked an assistant in a grey overall.

I was going to request the first thing to hand, which turned out to be one of the oblong cardboard-boxes piled under a counter. But before I could open my mouth, and as if he had only asked this question out of old habit and already regretted it, this strange salesman, pointing to the entrance to Andco & Co., said to me, 'If it's about a job, ask there.'

Then he turned his back on me. I found myself out on the street again, feeling perplexed. Next door, where I tried again, I did not even have time to ask anything. An assistant, dressed just like the first one, had already appeared from the shadows to give me the same information.

'I'm not looking for a job. I'd like to buy one of those,' I said, not wanting to admit defeat, and very much at a loss to name the goods contained in the dusty cardboard-boxes piled under a counter.

Hesitating, as if with a sudden twinge of conscience, my interlocutor stammered, 'But . . . monsieur . . . as you well know, none of this is for sale . . . I couldn't tell you the price of these articles . . .'

Finally, he opened one of the boxes and held out to me the doll it contained.

'Besides, you can see as well as I can, these dolls aren't yet finished . . .'

'You're right,' I said stupidly, 'they don't have any eyes . . .'

But I had no sooner uttered this last word than the assistant rudely snatched the doll from my hands and replaced it in its packaging, then hurriedly put it back where it came from.

'All these shops are doubtless no more than subsidiaries of Andco & Co.?' I then asked, quite surprised.

This time the sales assistant looked at me, dumbfounded, before replying curtly, 'Doubtless!' and disappearing into the back of the shop. My question about a fact so obvious did not merit an answer, as far as he was concerned.

'But what about the hotel? And Edith?' I said to myself, as soon as I was outside again. The thoughts came crowding into my head, meeting and multiplying like the passers-by in the square. And suddenly it seemed to me that all those faces were no longer unfamiliar to me, that I had already passed them, on a staircase, in a corridor, or glimpsed them in the shadows. Those two, and those two, and that fellow – did they not all have exactly the same features, though in a younger version, as the old folk in the hotel?

Then I rushed down the first street that opened up in front of me and ran hell for leather straight ahead of me, with the sole idea of fleeing these walls, of breaking out of this circle in which I was trapped.

At a certain point, sensing that I was being followed, I turned round. A young girl threw herself into my arms. She was exhausted by running and if I had not held her up she would have collapsed at my feet. Her reddish hair, dishevelled by the wind, completely covered her childish face, and I caught its earthy smell. Very close by us, an old man was scratching with a home-made bow on a peculiar violin: it consisted of a broom and an empty tin-can that served as a resonance chamber. The extraordinarily shrill sharp sounds this musician drew from his instrument were heart-breaking. Passers-by occasionally threw a coin into the dish set at his feet, and I noticed the expression of smug satisfaction that then appeared on their faces. But we could not stay there. Women in housecoats, going to do their shopping, stopped to stare at us. Almost carrying the young stranger, I came to the entrance of a building site surrounded by a fence. We went in and, having stumbled among piles of rubble and rubbish, found shelter under some temporary construction. I tried to allay the frenzy I could see on the young girl's face. Her extremely bright, brown eyes had a disquieting stare and yet did not settle on anything. Occasionally a brief smile enlivened her features, but they would immediately resume their intent expression.

'She's mad . . .' I thought with a certain anxiety. Indeed, everything about her behaviour betrayed madness . . . 'And mute as well!' I added, realizing that nothing succeeded in drawing her out of her silence. All of a sudden she draped her arms round my neck and offered me her mouth, which was as soft and sweet as a ripe wild fruit. I planted only an innocent kiss on it and, determined to calm her fervour, I gathered her up in my arms to cradle her young body like that of a child. She immediately fell asleep. Then I laid her on the ground under a shelter of planks. A steady rain, falling on the abandoned objects around us, drowned out the noise of the city, enfolding her slumber and my agitation in a sound like that of the sea. Released from the anxiety that had made me flee the square, and although only a few yards from the hotel, I felt miles away from everything, alone with this young girl who had fallen from a distant star. Too soon, alas, slight stirrings, an indistinct murmur, the advance signs of her wakening, announced the end of this strange period of calm. Without ceasing to watch her, I hastened to conceal myself from her sight. She seemed to emerge slowly from a delightful dream, then, noticing her surroundings, she abruptly got to her feet, and in two or three light bounds over all kinds of building materials she was back in the street. A few seconds later I saw her tiny figure disappear beneath the drizzle, mingling with passers-by. That evening I informed Edith of my intention to leave the hotel.

I had a found a solution that would allow me to pursue my investigation, continue with Dr Fohat's treatment, and at the same time tell Edith of my determination never to see things as she did. Since every house in the square, and the hotel too, belonged to Andco and Co., all I had to do was to ask the personnel department for permission to sleep not at the hotel any more but in some corner of that vast organization's offices or workshops, under a counter, for example, or in a lift-cage. So, by a strange aberration of my moral instincts, I, who disapproved of my colleagues' activities, who was aware of the odious trade in which my bosses dealt, instead of shunning the den where their crimes were probably perpetrated, was bent on never leaving it. I felt I could associate with the worst scoundrels without becoming like them, paddle in the same cesspool without being splattered. I felt that the same force impelling me to acquaint myself with all the evil going on would always prevent the foulness from affecting me too. That very evening, in recognition of my good services, I obtained permission to sleep on the premises of my workplace. What blundering and needless to-ing and fro-ing I was saving myself by this! From now on, everything would be simple. It would not take me long to discover the unifying thread connecting all my conjectures. It was in this happy frame of mind that I packed my togs. Oh, I did not have much in the way of luggage. Thanks to the empty pill-boxes, I had a place for some of my savings. Of the rest, I made a bundle tied with string, which I hid at the bottom of my suitcase. Walking past my land-lady's office, I thought I saw some twitching of the pleated curtains over the door.

The cubby-hole where I was to sleep in future served as a cupboard for brooms, cloths, and feather dusters. I installed a mattress on the floor, and once that was done, proceeded to unpack my belongings. Catastrophe! On the way over, I had broken my spec-tacles that were jammed in my suitcase. This acci-dent seemed a bad omen, although the glasses were hardly any use to me any more. A few minutes later, having taken my daily pill, I settled down to go to sleep. But when sleep did not come, I thought of the time when I had only to place the lenses over my eyes to be plunged immediately into a salutary repose. And I ended up regretting the early period of my stay in the hotel. When I had no knowledge of what was going on around me, everything seemed easy! I had one sole purpose, one sole desire, and forgot that every other one was satisfied in pursuit of it. Bah! Those days were long gone. Multiplying questions added an interest to my life that it did not have then. What a lot of good answers I had since found to a great many problems! It was only the loss of my spectacles that set me thinking about the time when my personality was so weak. That evening I wanted so much to sleep, only to sleep! And I just could not.

Having achieved so much, I was now unable to satisfy this very modest desire.

My restlessness gave rise to chaotic impressions. Was that not the sound of multitudes blocked out by these walls behind which I remained miraculously isolated – safe perhaps, but in what state of dereliction? Where did the gleams of light filtering through the gaps in the wooden partitions come from? The night wore on, filled with anxiety, and I sensed the moment returning when I would have to leap to my brooms, cloths and feather dusters, without having been able to relax. After several hours' wakefulness, I got up, determined to do anything to get some sleep. The foreman, through whom I had been granted permission to stay in this cubby-hole, had given me a thousand instructions, including that of not emerging from my quarters during the night. But since I had been seeking out my colleagues' confidences, I had continually lied, breaking with one of them promises made to another. Going back on my word once more would not matter. And besides, why and of what was I trying to clear myself? Was not my only intention, at that moment, to take a few steps in the corridor, merely a few steps, so as to be able to sleep?

Just as awareness of dreaming, while dreaming, begins with the certainty of being wide awake, so awareness of the marvellous, when awake, starts from the moment when reality unduly oppresses you. As soon as the door of my cubby-hole closed behind me, I had the sudden feeling of having locked away a part of myself for ever, within those four walls, along with the brooms and feather dusters. The fellow now

groping his way forward in the corridor was no longer the same person who had just been tossing and
turning on a pallet in the hope of getting some sleep.
Totally awake now, this brand-new me let himself be
carried towards a mystery he had some inkling of
without yet being able to grasp it. All was dark, but
it was replete darkness, a living darkness. The building I believed to be deserted was filled with a secret
murmur, like the breathing of a thousand breathers.
Behind its corridors, and staircases on which I stumbled, behind its walls that I ran my hands over without recognizing them, broke the swell of a thousand
dreams, a deeper, duller sound more terrible than the
human tide surging all day long over the paving
stones in the square.

For how long did I proceed like this? When my
eyes grew accustomed to the dark and were at last
able to guide me – and the glimmer of light ahead
was like a large formless angel come to lead me – I
did not recognize any of my surroundings. No doubt,
in my blind progress I had gone beyond the bounds
that my work allowed me to move within during the
day. I was making my way through a series of rooms
of every dimension, leading into each other: some so
long they were really like corridors; others, small and
square, getting bigger and bigger in succession, until
they reached the size of a barrack-room, and then
getting smaller and smaller again. There were rect-
angular rooms, octagonal rooms, and some very odd
shapes, full of nooks and corners. But this progres-
sion of differing sizes always gave the impression
that, should the necessity arise, the rooms could

easily be nested inside each other. The doors of all these interconnecting rooms must have opened in front of me automatically, or perhaps they did not exist? I could not say, so taken up was I with watching and listening to what was going on in each one. Sometimes these rooms looked as though diminished by distance, reduced to the proportions of a model stage set, but in which every object, every living being was as clearly visible as if it had been painted with the precision of a miniaturist. There were other times, when on the contrary I saw them as an ant's eye must see things, as though through an enormous magnifying glass, looking huge, their confines lost in a haze, and the things or beings they contained then floating about, as vague and indeterminate as clouds.

Over here, on rows of beds no bigger than coffins, lay sleeping children. No breath escaped their lips, but occasionally one of them, in the sole sign of life, would raise a transparent little hand, which remained momentarily suspended over its slumber like a bulbous flower that no sooner blossomed than wilted. And over there, extremely beautiful women, fascinating in their sleep, dreamed aloud, repeating the same question, which unanswered, over and over again, like a lesson learned by heart, but with the terrible accents of passion. Elsewhere, slender-limbed young people with slight torsos were also stretched out, sound asleep, but the mark of an injury partially disfigured their faces. And yet elsewhere, virgins, their bodies wrapped in their long hair, lay side by side, sometimes elegantly entangled. The lustre of a brow, the whiteness of a breast suddenly gleamed in this confusion like the morning star. What was surprising about all these recumbent beings was both the extreme weariness and anxiety on their faces. They looked as if they had been struck down in their prime and, dead to a serene life on earth, were living through a second existence, full of torment. For they were all young, with none of the usual signs of age marring their faces. I tried to get closer to identify them, but I kept coming up against a kind of invisible wall, through which they seemed to recede into infinity, just as I was about to touch them. I had to retreat before they would resume their original position and I could see them again. An occasional word rang out, a call or response, reverberating through the many rooms. But its echo would fall back into silence, like the momentarily suspended hand of the child.

The same tedious range of human specimens – that was word for them – recurred in all these rooms. I was expecting one of this multitude to sit up and gaze at me with eyes that were not the eyes of sleep, but I was disappointed. To tell the truth, their stillness was only apparent. When I watched closely, I noticed that from time to time it was punctuated by an almost imperceptible unrest. Limbs writhed or crumpled under invisible tortures, hands opened, like predatory aquatic plants waiting their opportunity, sweating brows sought a coolness that was not there, muscles tensed, taut nerves suddenly slackened, all in nightmarish slow-motion. But if I managed to tear my gaze away from this ferment, I could see very well I had been the victim of an illusion: all was silent and still. And I then hurried on, with slight dread, as though passing through the deserted rooms of a waxworks museum.

After this sequence of rooms, I came to a spiral staircase descending to the floor below. Still advancing like a sleepwalker, I found myself, when I got to the bottom, in a huge space with concrete walls. In the centre of this space, machines quietly hummed. There was no attendant running them, but the manifold actions of rods, turbines and gear-wheels nevertheless gave rise to an impression of total security. A countless number of goods-lifts worked ceaselessly, automatically filling and empty-ing with the aid of tip-trays on which I was horrified to see shroud-covered human figures appearing and disappearing, gobbled up by enormous mechanical mouths. All this virtually silent activity took place in an atmosphere of cleanliness, even luxury, so shiny were the polished copper and nickel. I staggered past the bare featureless walls, like some lost shadow, sole survivor of this morgue that trundled out its corpses – what else could they be? – before subjecting them to some mysterious operation that my mind refused to comprehend.

An enormous pipe ran across the ceiling above an escalator, probably intended for the missing work-force of this model factory, which carried me to the threshold of a huge, totally deserted laboratory. There, my attention was immediately caught by some kind of mannequin or inert automaton, lying on a table, whose upper body was cased in a curious carapace of greenish lead. By contrast, its legs were totally human in appearance. Elsewhere, various coloured liquids flowed and mingled in transparent retorts and test-tubes. After long maceration in every shape of recipient, all these ingredients, passing through a complex system of tubes, eventually combined into a dark paste resembling tar. This viscous substance was left to set in a row of cement vats that extended out of sight in a store room adjoining the laboratory.

What amazed me most, perhaps by quirk of professional interest, was how spick and span all these rooms were, whose existence I had until now been unaware of. Previously under the illusion of being the only handyman assigned to cleaning duty, I now realized with suppressed anxiety that during the day there must be whole teams working here in relays to attend to all these rooms, machines and instruments. The few workshops and offices I had to look after represented only a tiny part of this huge establishment. And until that moment I had been living in ignorance of all this. Thousands of men had the same scruples as I did. Like me, in all probability, they felt exempt of responsibility, while pushing their brooms and polishing the brass. And the machine operated all by itself in the nocturnal silence without one speck of dust threatening to hamper its workings; the machine operated all by itself, because of them.

I climbed more staircases, wandered along more corridors, and at last came to a dead-end room, to which all the others undoubtedly led. Entering it, I had the strange sensation of recognizing where I was. There was a bright light in here, as if the employees working in this room had just that moment left and were going to return any minute. Their grey overalls were still hanging beside the door. Between two rows of counters were packing cases of all sizes stacked on top of each other. I went over to them with curiosity. But there was no indication of their contents. Then, suddenly seized with a kind of frenzy, I grabbed a tool lying on the table, and breaking the wooden slates and tearing the cardboard, I ripped open one of these mysterious packing cases. A multitude of little boxes cascaded onto the ground, and I saw bursting out of some of them round blackish pills similar to the ones I took every evening. Bending over these boxes, I read with amazement: 'Dr Fohat's Pills'. Where was I? My vision blurred under the blinding light. Just as anyone in a fever longs to quench their thirst, I felt the sudden need for darkness. When I switched off the light, the gloom was like a soothing bath. All these discoveries had exhausted me, as if I had been racing for my very life.

But on one whole side of the room, a pale glow, coming from outside, seems to creep towards me. I go over and, drawing back one of the curtains from behind which this dawn light filters, I uncover a big glass window. And through this window I am not surprised to see – for I have at last guessed where I am – the window of my old room. So, in wandering through this labyrinth, I have come all the way round the square. The circle is complete. The big glass window that so intrigued me in the past is no longer a mystery. There is no mystery any more. Since I first entered Dr Fohat's surgery, I have never ceased to belong to Andco & Co. Perhaps my own decisions were nothing but fantasies, permitted, not to say suggested, by will of this far from innocuous company.

And yet, even though I felt there was nothing more that night that could be revealed to me, a whole aspect of my adventure remained obscure. As I reflected on this, still striving to understanding, my eyes were fixed on my window. Slowly, the wan light of dawn blanched the slatted surface of its closed shutters. And after a moment I thought I detected a shadow wavering on that pale screen. Then leaning forward to peer up at the cause of this shadow, I saw Edith's corpse, caught in the high-voltage cables above my room, like an enormous night-bird pinned against the sky.

THE AVENUE

Water blurs things, distorts appearances, attaches the moon to the drowned man's eyes. It tosses its slimy fish into the heavens, makes the birds of the sky swim in its silt. Paramount of forces that blend, and dissolve, water only banishes demons and charms and evil spells the better to swallow us up. Water spiders, skeletons of the stars caught in its perfidious nets. It runs and flows away, hands cannot hold it. The quicksilver of its gushing forth changes, when stagnant, into heavy ink, a mirror for beautiful women and refuge of the hopeless.

Reason only serves to justify our impulses. It is the useless pennant proclaiming in the wind, 'I am the one responsible for the movements of all this bulk beneath me, I am the captain of the ship . . .', while the sails swell and strain in silence. After the discovery of Edith's suicide, the arguments that only the day before had shored up the case for my continuing to live among the people of the square suddenly collapsed. And I found another hundred, another thousand reasons why I should leave. This regimen did not suit me. I would go and tell Dr Fohat. He had erred, in my regard, in imagining I could be kept in the dark while being cured. Taking the steps four at a time coming out of Andco & Co., thoroughly excited by this change in my life, I cried, 'No more treatment!' just like a child chanting, 'Long live the holidays!' But out in the street, I almost collided with one of the oldest and most trusty employees, arriving for work, as he did every morning. He mumbled a few words I did not catch, although they were addressed to me.

The person who thinks himself immured in his wretchedness has only his own inadequacy to blame. A 'beyond' is always accessible. A taxi was passing, and I asked the driver to take me to Dr Fohat's. But he had never heard of a doctor by that name. So I told him with some irritation to take me to an optician, preferably an ophthalmologist. He replied that he had never in his life needed spectacles, and therefore did not know of a single optician.

'Take me wherever you like,' I then shouted at him, 'as long as it's away from here!'

He looked at me as if dealing with a madman, but nevertheless did not refuse to take me and my luggage on board. It was only when I was seated in the back of the car that it occurred to me that this was the first taxi I had ever seen in the neighbourhood. We drove fast and it only took a moment to reach a long avenue. This completely straight road allowed my driver to go even faster. The houses and trees flashed by so quickly that it was impossible to distinguish them. Were they still trees and houses? Not at all scared, but on the contrary slightly exhilarated by our speedy progress, as the number of kilometres between the square and myself rose, the more cheerful I became, regardless of the danger this reckless fellow was placing me in. Of all my anxieties of the preceding weeks, I was left with only one small concern: I should have asked that old employee who had spoken to me for Dr Fohat's address. Perhaps that's what he had tried to tell me? In any case, he must know of him. How crazy to have gone off like that! Who could tell me now? But the further we went, the more the thrill of speed effaced even this worry.

When my taxi finally slowed down, the avenue seemed broader, although just as straight and unrelieved. At that moment, in fact, we were making a clever turn off it, into another broad avenue with lots of luxurious vehicles travelling in every direction. But on paying closer attention, I realized this turn had taken place only in my imagination. It was the same avenue as before, although now thronged with an elegantly dressed crowd. The buildings had lavish window displays and all had at least five storeys, each with a balcony. My taxi seemed almost shabby in this setting, this brilliant hubbub. It had been driving desperately slowly for the past several minutes, as if out of petrol. Finally, it stopped. I felt a kind of relief. With a farewell wave to my driver, I was about to head off as quickly as possible. But a volley of abuse brought me hurriedly back to my point of departure: this impatient fellow was claiming his due. I hastily reassured him, drawing a bundle of notes out of one of my suitcases. I had been living for so long without money, I had completely lost the habit of using it. What unforgivable absentmindedness! And how was I to explain that to this lout? To keep him quiet, I gave him a handsome tip (in this elegant neighbourhood, I must not forget in future that money would be essential at all times.) Many people who looked much smarter than I gazed at me admiringly when they saw me handing out a tip like that so casually. So, to tell the truth, I was not unhappy about this incident. It afforded me a new and agreeable experience. Squaring my shoulders, I strode off, to give the impression of having a great many things to attend to, or being very purposeful.

The splendid shopfronts glittered on either side of the avenue. I shot only a few hasty glances at them, deferring till later the curiosity they aroused in me.

Every now and then, the entrance of some sumptuous hotel encroached on the pavement, like a
boat-landing. But I dared not sit down in one of
those armchairs offered for the repose of passers-by.
Would I have been capable of talking to the waiters
with sufficient unselfconsciousness, as I saw others
doing? Such ease amid luxury terrified me a little.
When only yesterday I was proudly accepting the
most humiliating tasks, it felt almost indecent to be
venturing into these palaces today. I was so well
embarked on a life of poverty! From the age of
twelve, I had to struggle to earn my living, and this
precocious experience of hardship had speckled my
heart with the fox-marks of rebellion. No hope then
of escaping: my life would be like those around me,
wretched and peevish. And now, indirectly, almost
against my will, thanks to Dr Fohat's treatment I
had acquired some of the privileges of wealth. I
would never have thought it possible to accumulate
so much money, in such a short time, simply by not
using any! Here was I, once unable to enter a public
place without blushing, and just the day before a
poor shameful wretch carrying swill for dogs, now
strolling at my ease down this smart avenue, the
equal of these people whose company I would only
have scorned yesterday, out of resentful envy. I needed to adapt to this new situation, to undertake a
readjustment of my scale of values. I could not
plunge straight into this new world. To reconcile my
lingering scruples and the undeniable satisfactions to
my pride that, I had the feeling, the prestige of
wealth would bring me, I hoped to find modest lodg-

ings in some little side-street without going too far from this area. But I walked on and on, passing elegant women whom I looked at more and more boldly, seeing that they sought my gaze and their eyes were no longer filled with indifference, as in the past. I walked on, without any more humble street presenting itself to me. What I sometimes mistook for a street corner would turn out to be just the entrance of a garage or a cinema. And in the end I had to face up to it: this avenue had no side-streets running off it. Before and behind me, it vanished into the horizon. It was apparently impossible to get off it or come back on to it without returning to the beginning or going on to the end.

Hunger led me to push open the door of a restaurant. All eyes fixed on me when I entered, then quickly turned away, but with feigned inattention. There was a woman carrying dishes. She looked tired. In fact, she must have been very tired. She was being as quick as she could to satisfy the people she had to serve. Each time, she had to descend a staircase to the distant kitchens, then climb up again, with her hands full, carrying desserts and soups, then hand some slips to the cash-desk, and finally rush over to the customers. There were a lot of women like her in this restaurant, and also some elderly waiters who somehow managed to joke while working out the bill on the tablecloth. The excessively white napkins left a persistent fluff on people's clothes. No doubt many came to eat here because it was inexpensive. I soon realized that customers leaving the room did not take the door on to the avenue, but a little staircase

71

probably leading to an exit known only to its regulars. I imagined this exit gave access to a more modest neighbourhood and I vowed to do likewise when I had finished my meal, already rejoicing in the idea of at last finding in some quiet street a room to suit my simple tastes. But the moment I rose from the table several young people surrounded me, notebook and pen in hand, and began to question me. I was quite ill at ease, especially as everyone in the room at this point was staring at me without inhibition. These onlookers, I now saw, were fairly coarse types. Most of their faces bore the marks of servility, sometimes of the basest kind. The impression of congenital imbecility that characterized them, the vacuous admiration in their eyes restored a bit of my confidence. But I could not understand my interviewers' questions, nor why they were talking to me. One of them asked me to autograph a photograph, another had me sign a publicity leaflet about an elixir to enhance the beauty of one's eyes, a third was desperately keen to know what brand of shaving soap I used. Bewildered, I at first replied evasively, explaining to them that I had just arrived in this neighbourhood and asking where I might find lodgings. But they seemed no more able to understand the meaning of my words than I could understand the meaning of theirs. This seemed not to matter to them and did not prevent them from covering their pads with notes. Then, emboldened and caught up in the game by the sight of the circle around me growing more and more dense, I began to boast of imaginary feats, inventing some absurd story of which I was the hero.

The more improbable what I told them, the happier they seemed. At last I managed to escape, but forgetting, in the excitement, to take the little back door as I had intended, I found myself back in the midst of the avenue's hustle and bustle.

After walking for a long while, I finally decided to enter one of the luxurious hotels set to tempt passers-by. Everything went as well as it possibly could, and I quickly realized how I should behave in this new environment. As soon as I was alone, I put away safely the wads of money in my suitcase. The sight of such a large amount reminded me of my debt to Edith. But since she could no longer be paid back, why should I worry about it? I could not blame myself for her death! Her realization that she had failed to fulfil her destiny was all that had brought her to that extreme. If I owed her anything, it was only the cost of my lodgings, an account which I never felt I had squared, despite all the assurances she lavished on me relating to that matter. But to settle that debt, I would have had to return to the hotel, and perhaps fall into the hands of its new manageress. No doubt this replacement was young and pretty? I shuddered at the thought of the danger this would put me in. No, there could be no question of my going back there. The atmosphere that now surrounded me was so different that all those events, although still recent, seemed to have taken place in another world. Reflecting on them only made me realize how easy it would have been, had I thought of it earlier, not to be burdened with this slight remorse. These hard-earned savings of mine were nothing to be ashamed of. In this wealthy neighbourhood where living without means would have been impossible, all my old scruples began to disperse. And why should I have retained any scruples? So many others led their lives without wondering where the money they lived on came from? Better still, they congratulated and prided themselves on the objects they bought, as if there were any merit in that. But had I myself not been crazy enough to believe in the efficacy of a treatment that subjected me to menial toil, when it would have been so easy to free myself earlier, so easy to take the decision, before being forced by events, to leave the square and its deeply disquieting territories?

Behind a seeming complicatedness and frivolity, the way of life of the people on the avenue entailed only two or three ritual activities, but ones that no one ever transgressed. The magnetic centre of their lives was the avenue, which explained the continual to-and-fro on the broad pavements, day and night. Since this conduit of traffic had no beginning or end – I mean, the beginning and end were so far away that no one dreamt of even envisaging the possibility of reaching them – it could be said that these pedestrians never went anywhere. Despite their apparent frenzy, they remained where they were, condemned to stagnation. As for the many fast-travelling cars, everyone, including their occupants, had come to realize that they only drove at such speed to prove to a countless number of engineers and mechanics the accuracy of their calculations and their matchless skill. They always returned to their numerous garages along the avenue. Yet there was a way of escaping from this bind and getting away from these wealthy surroundings. Every house had in its common parts a more or less secret door leading on to little streets outside that were silent and deserted. Most of the inhabitants of the avenue never used these clandestine exits. They had no desire to, indeed they seemed unaware of their very existence, and did not know there might be some other way of life than frequenting those nearby meeting places in the avenue. At first I often ventured forth along these little streets, needing a change of air. I could not help thinking, also, that some time or other I really must try to get back to Dr Fohat this way. But their quietness and seclusion so violently contrasted with the bustling life of the avenue that I, too, quickly lost the habit of going there. Such lack of animation could be explained. These little streets were inhabited by all the staff from the shops, institutions and establishments of all kinds that stood on the main thoroughfare, and these employees did not get home until evening, so tired they were ready to drop. The rest of their lives was spent in their place of work. The people they worked for, the real inhabitants of the avenue – of whom I was one, although by accident, admittedly – spent most of their time going in and out of shops, restaurants and cinemas. They could not remain still. They no sooner arrived in a place than they were hurrying away from it as quickly as possible. The sole site they favoured was the avenue itself and its broad pavements. There, going round and round, as it were, in desperation, almost running, they passed, overtook, crowded and jostled each other all day long, in a hurry to arrive no one, not even they themselves, knew where.

A bright, comfortable room was my home. Its large windows looked out over the avenue at the spot where, I thought, the taxi from the square had deposited me one day. In reality, I was miles from there, as I had walked all afternoon before finding lodgings. But since the avenue was always just the same, I had probably forgotten how far I had come. Anyway, this apartment suited me, so why should I have looked any further? Why should I have retraced my steps? There was only one shadow over my contentment: the precariousness of these new circumstances. It was all very well my living in a kind of flux, a continual levity – this was dancing with my eyes closed so as not to see the chasm that was going to engulf me. Yes, my life at that time was like a dance, and that is perhaps why I have so little recollection of it. Yet, of the countless things that filled it, what was to predominate was the unfamiliar and bizarre sensation, experienced on my arrival, of being an object of wonder to those around me. It seemed to me then that it was only the hugeness of the tip I had given to my driver that attracted the attention of passers-by. But afterwards I had to admit that no one had noticed the money. It was my self more than my actions that was the object of their curiosity. Now I could not take a step without seeing them turn to stare at me. I had already been exposed to such indiscretion, of the same insistent kind, the day I came out of the ophthalmologist's, with my package under my arm. But now my hands were always empty and I wondered what it was about me that could so draw attention. Women being unable to hold their tongues, I would sometimes hear, when I passed close by them, an exclamation I did not pay much heed to at first, but that, by repetition, finally impressed itself on me: 'Oh, lovely eyes!' 'Did you see those eyes?' 'What splendid eyes!'

I could not believe they were talking about mine. In what way had they become so remarkable? But bent over my mirror in the evening, I was obliged to concede that, to my amazement, my eyes had changed. Their oval shape was slightly larger, and a darker iris enhanced the depth of my gaze. My eyes were indisputably handsome. They were magnificent.

I spent the night pondering on this peculiar development. This transformation of my eyes was surely one of the first effects of the treatment, an effect that only manifested itself after I had left the square, and which might never have manifested itself had I not done so. This outcome was not contrary to the one anticipated. It was simply different. Perhaps later my eyesight would improve, just as the appearance of my eyes had recently improved, of which I had clear proof. It was all closely related. But for now a cure was out of the question. It was too late to resume the treatment. At dawn I fell asleep and dreamed of the many adventures this abnormality was going to lead me into. But when I woke up, none of this childishness remained with me. How could the fact of having lovely eyes change my destiny? Of course, I would have preferred to have my trouble cured. I would have much preferred to be able to see properly! I would gladly have given all my money to be able to find Dr Fohat's address again. But no one in this neighbourhood had ever heard mention of this name. If the person I asked pricked up his ears as though suddenly interested, a total indifference, as it were, just as quickly overcame his momentary attention, and I had to give up the attempt to get the least information out of him. Whenever I spoke to a woman, she at once fell into a kind of swoon before my eyes, and I had to put up strong resistance so as not to let myself be drawn into forgetting the point of my question. Fortunately, I was beginning to know how to defend myself against self-conceit. But the ease of my conquests locked me into a circle of vicissitudes that I was powerless to break out of. Nevertheless, I felt I was wasting the prime of my life; that the months and years were passing, bringing me only an insubstantial and superficial contentment. I wished I could harness myself to some task that would have saved me from this dissipation, that I could take an interest in works of art or literature, but my poor eyesight prevented me from spending much time with my nose in a book. While wasting most of my time, I sometimes had the impression that I was behaving exactly as if I had been granted the right to two lives, and that this one was a trial run, a small supplementary existence in which I had been given the privilege, in the meantime, of living a little like other people. From the most innocuous accidents of fate, infinite complications would arise at every moment, setting me on courses that went completely against my nature.

That newspaper vendor beneath my windows! It was inevitable: every time I sat down at my table to write, his deafening cries turned my brain into a soft paste in which ideas remained gummed. One day, driven to distraction, I went flying out into the street, roughed up the pest, and threw his beastly bundle of baloney into the nearest gutter. The next day two gentlemen came to congratulate me. My courageous stand against their adversary had, it seemed, been noticed. I protested, but they took my disclaimers for modesty, and as a matter of course enrolled me into a party I knew nothing about.

Sometimes, having made one false move, you commit another to justify yourself, then yet another to justify this peculiar behaviour. Hoping for a better hearing, I subsequently attended meetings and took an active part in assemblies. Whenever I spoke, it was only to demonstrate the fundamental misconception of my position, to sort out the confusion that had brought me there, in short to explain that all I wanted, and all I had ever wanted, was my own peace and quiet. But such was the superstition of the crowd that, to their ears, the meaning of my words was of no importance; all that mattered was the fervour and conviction with which they were expressed. My eyes especially, in spite of myself, fascinated them, rendering useless my appeals to their reason. And with one misapprehension leading to another, I who abhorred all contact with others in general and politics in particular, soon became one of the 'leaders' (that, I think, was their jargon) of the party in question.

While getting ever deeper into this paradoxical situation, I eventually realized, however, that I was actually committing my life to a course that was contrary to its nature and ambitions. And one day I resolved to abandon all these people and the hope of justifying myself with them, by totally avoiding them. I later learned they had dragged my name through the mud after all this, and continued to regard me as a traitor to their cause, a turncoat, an hypocrite, and I don't know what else besides!

I consoled myself for this misadventure with romantic liaisons, mostly of short duration. They left me with nothing but the bitterness of renewed disillusionment. Always, after my initial enthusiasm convinced me that at last the best of myself was going to be able to flourish, I endlessly prevaricated to find out if the woman I had chosen was really worth the trouble of my dedicating to her this unique part of my being. How complicated it was to then part company with the woman I had deceived for all that time by deceiving myself. Sometimes, amazed not to be alone in bed, I would waken – perhaps I had not really yet fallen asleep: what hour of the night was it? – overwhelmed by the strength of my joy. All these riches mine, this wonderful body, this face, radiant with youth! I would never have believed that the sense of possession could be so absolute. And I had only to say the word for this happiness to be not just momentary but lifelong. With what passionate ardour I prepared myself to say this word. But the face of the woman I had just made my mistress would emerge from the dark and I would see it in broad daylight. And it was as if this stark brightness on her features had suddenly purged them of my aberration. I saw this face as it would be in twenty years' time. And, shuddering, I thought I heard a tired voice, cracked with age, muttering words full of ghastly tenderness.

A peculiar venture that striped me of my last illusion was to cure me for ever of this senseless pursuit. A cinema producer offered me a remunerative contract, which I only accepted, in exasperation, on condition that I played the part blindfolded. Naturally this gentleman laughed in my face. Then I proposed making the film at my expense, but wearing an invisible mask or some other device that would replace my eyes with glass eyes. This experiment would reveal whether it was only my eyes that the public really admired in me. I wished to owe my fame to personal ability and not to this physical attribute that I was beginning to find oppressive, no doubt because I had done nothing to acquire it. The day this film was premiered I was in the darkened theatre, incognito. It goes without saying, I was expecting it to be a total flop, although deep down inside I was hoping for a great success. But I had reckoned without the stupidity of the crowd, to whom I was no stranger. When the character I played appeared on the screen, the whole house sat up eagerly.

'Oh, what lovely eyes! What lovely eyes!' everyone cried around me.

I longed to convey my disgust to these blind fools. 'They're glass eyes! Can't you see, they're glass eyes!' But what was the point? I might have fallen victim to their frenzy as soon as they recognized me, and I was tired of these histrionics. I fled, having lowered my hat over my brow, leaving that masked shadow of myself still flickering on the screen, feeding their stupidity.

Would the subterfuge I had resorted to in a sphere so unreal as that of cinemas where people go looking for dream-pastures, perhaps succeed better in wide-awake life without the greasepaint? This line of thought gave rise one morning to the very simple idea of wearing dark glasses, as before. Since I was incapable of imposing on myself the discipline to set my life back on its fundamental course, perhaps I would regain my tranquillity by this exterior means? Cheerful and excited, I got dressed and rushed off to find an optician. Was not my first instinct, on leaving the square, to get myself taken, if not to Dr Fohat, to someone who sold spectacles? So, all these years of public life, which had left me with the taste of dust that comes after a series of disappointments, could have been avoided if that blasted driver had taken me where I wanted to go in the first place! I surely would not have failed to buy a pair of glasses to replace Dr Fohat's from this optician. And all the misunderstandings that my eyes had given rise to would not have occurred. It only takes a second for our destiny to deviate at any moment if we are not vigilant.

Wandering along the straight avenue, looking up at the shop signs, I arrived at the point where the taxi from the square had dropped me off. And I suddenly noticed, in large letters on the facade of one of the imposing buildings: EYE SPECIALIST. Going closer, I read with amazement, above the entrance: FORMER PRACTICE OF A. FOHAT. Without knowing it – but was it really the case that he did not know? – the driver all that time ago had brought me exactly where I wanted to go. But he failed to tell me. My attention not having been drawn to it, I had walked past this building that chance brought me back to today. He might just as well have driven me miles away from here, since I remained unaware of it. The very small fact of my ignorance for a while transformed my life. And how many times since then had I passed in front of this doorway without seeing it, because I failed to keep looking, because I thought Dr Fohat was far away. It had not occurred to me that he might have a practice here with numerous wealthy clients. If I had only raised my eyes, I could have seen his name, that remained deep in my heart, up there in shiny letters, every time I passed by! But of fate's intentions and opportunities, nothing was yet lost. It was just all this time that had gone by that was lost, lost for ever.

A great many clients were waiting in the room I entered. Heavy draperies and modern stained-glass windows gave this hall the atmosphere of a first-class lounge on a transatlantic passenger ship for millionaires. Thick carpets silenced the general coming-and-going and, affable and conspiratorial, the employees dancing attendance on the public seemed to understand from mere lip-movements what each person wanted to say. A slender youth dressed as a page-boy came and handed me a number engraved on a brass tag and smilingly invited me, in a murmur, to take a seat. This I did with good grace, for the deep armchair, covered with the same thick tapestry that was hung on the walls was a genuine temptation to my weariness. I crossed my legs with a nonchalant casualness that was not lacking in affectation, and letting my eyes wander over the elegant throng so much in harmony with the luxurious surroundings, I began to think of Dr Fohat's former premises, of the filthy staircase and its odours, and the gloomy and foul-smelling courtyard that served as an entrance.

'There's something to be said for working as an ophthalmologist,' I said to myself.

But I quickly realized the unsoundness of my reasoning. In fact, it could very well be that Dr Fohat had died in poverty, and that this palace, inhabited by his successor, had never belonged to him. Indeed, it was quite possible that he had nothing to do with this extravagant luxury. No doubt, to the end he had remained unaware of it. Someone else, speculating on his reputation, exploiting his clients, had grown rich on his legacy. These thoughts, however, did not deprive me of one iota of my complacency, and I must have dozed off, lulled by the many whispers in this plush and comfortable place.

I was wakened by a light tap on the shoulder. The white hand of another flunkey, dressed like the page at the entrance, called me back to reality. It was my turn to proceed to a room that was smaller than the first although still of imposing dimensions, and also with thick hangings on the walls. Standing motionless on either side of a large door with carved panelling were two guards dressed up like heralds in an operetta, each holding a halberd. All this pomp had no great effect on me and I was about to doze off again when a shrill ringing sounded. The two panels of the huge door opened and I finally entered the ophthalmologist's office.

I saw a giant of sorts with a shrewish face. His black eyes, several centimetres from the ceiling, pinned me to the ground from above. I was not scared by this monster, having noticed at once this abnormal height was only due to a pair of stilts, ineptly concealed beneath a long dressing-gown. Intending to take a step towards me, he was hampered by this scaffolding and it was only thanks to a quick jump that he did not go sprawling at my feet. The cumbersome garment and wooden poles fell in a pitiful heap in a corner. I had before me a small wiry man, whose rat-like eyes continued to stare at me, not without a degree of absurdity. But this individual must have believed himself to be above all absurdity. He addressed me as if nothing had happened:

'Marcel Adrien, take a seat!'

85

That he should know my name did not surprise me, since I had spelled it out to the doorman on entering.

'The tricks only impress simple-minded folk, unused to this kind of bluff,' I thought. And I sat down with the intention of not allowing myself to be impressed.

The little man – he really was very small – sat cross-legged on his desk.

'Marcel Adrien,' he resumed, 'I am very familiar with your case . . .'

Yes, it was more or less the same formula. The fellow did not bring anything original to his predecessor's method. He was very probably going to refer to my file being locked in one of the large drawers lining the walls from floor to ceiling. But none of this interested me any more; it did not work. As successful as my interview with Dr Fohat had been in awakening many emotional responses in me the same words uttered by this little fellow now seemed empty of meaning. The entrance ritual had instilled me with a sense of unease I could not shake off. The very tone of this interview, by its studiedness, its falseness, set me on edge.

'Silence!' I suddenly shouted. 'Do you think I'm taken in by your humbug? In any case, I didn't come here to listen to it, but to buy a pair of glasses, do you understand, a pair of dark glasses, the darkest you have in the way of glasses!'

At these words my interlocutor took a frog-leap backwards, and rummaging in a drawer he began to mutter, 'Fine, fine, sir, I'm at your command . . .', or something along those lines.

Finally he popped up through a flap in the middle of the table, waving under my nose a pair of glasses that might have served as a street-sign to his establishment. They spanned no less than fifty centimetres. I had to burst out laughing at the sight of them. And seeing there was nothing to be gained from this peculiar ophthalmologist, or one so self-styled, I was about to walk out, when, thinking better of it, I rushed at the impertinent fellow with clenched fists.

So, he took the liberty of aping his master! He found it amusing to make a mockery of his clients' ailments in this way! Well, we should see about that! And grabbing him by the tie, I shook him like a plum-tree.

He struggled wildly and tried to shout, 'Leave me alone, leave me alone!' But the words were choked by his stiff collar, and all that his throat managed to emit was a sound rather like a croak.

His eyes, like frantic marbles, no longer tried to hypnotize me. When I had satisfied my rage, without releasing him I in turn stared at him until his poodle gaze allowed itself to be pinned by mine. There must have been something formidable in my eyes, for the usurper's face became covered in sweat while I held him like this. And I was not surprised to hear myself asking him, as if this question were the supreme expression of my anger, 'Is Dr Fohat dead, then? Can he possibly be dead?'

Thereupon, I felt ashamed of my behaviour. Letting my victim fall back into the armchair, I slowly wiped my brow, leaning back on the desk, patiently waiting for his reply. It came only after a long pause during which I felt, watching that hunted face in front of mine, as if my own life were ebbing away drop by drop.

'I'll have to go on waiting like this for ages,' I said to myself, 'with this ghoul before my eyes, and this opaque dimness all around. For ages and ages I shan't be able to do anything but wait and wait . . .'

But Dr Fohat's successor had no sooner opened his mouth than my breathing became deeper, more regular, and I felt all thoughts that were not of hope and confidence depart from me.

Dr Fohat was not dead. And everyone considered it normal that this charlatan should assume the right to pass himself off as his successor! Indeed, there were many people who confused the real Dr Fohat with the man who was less than his shadow. How could it have been otherwise if the correct formalities were fulfilled in the transaction that secured the sale of the business and goodwill? No one now knew Dr Fohat, did not even know he existed, but 'Dr Fohat's successor' was installed in a prime location, making money hand over fist. I was shocked at such an outrage. Had not I myself momentarily believed he might be dead, and this ridiculous midget his sole representative? Now my hopes of finding him again, of speaking and listening to him again, revived. This deflated windbag had surely forgotten what had become of his predecessor. As I put the question to him, out of over-scrupulousness, I watched him grow flustered, and splutter, fearful of the return of my anger. Finally, taking advantage of a second's inattentiveness on my part, he disappeared from my sight, no doubt through a secret trap-door whose release-mechanism he had not until then been able to activate. So, having thus terrorized the master of the house, I was reduced to politely questioning the operetta guards standing around outside the door.

'Dr Fohat? No, sorry . . .' they replied in chorus.

In vain I questioned all the employees in turn, bluntly, with no respect for whatever fancy-dress they might be got up in. None of them knew Dr Fohat's address. Some thought he was dead; others said he had left the country; yet others that he must have been reincarnated in the body of their new boss. I went home, vowing to return the next day, and the following days, obsessed as I was by the idea of finding *him* again, of seeing *him*. The avenue had no appeal for me any more. Never had the insignificance of its inhabitants been so clearly apparent to me. My sole destination now was that monumental entrance, that sumptuous plush hall of murmurs. In that place alone I still stood some chance of hearing his name quietly mentioned.

Soon the employees paid no further attention to my presence. They seemed to have totally forgotten the day when I had been rather rude to them. Forbearance and forgiveness of offence were among the staff's obligations, listed among the watchwords of this establishment. But these pretentious flunkies had another way of taking their revenge: the scorn they poured on me, under cover of their unctuous manner and conventional politenesses. No matter how much I harassed them with questions the whole time, from the lift-boy to the overdressed cashier, they no longer regarded me as a serious client. The big boss, with his stilts, I preferred not to see again. If I did, how would I resist the pleasure of ramming his patter back down his throat again, once and for all? Knowing this individual to have set himself up in Dr Fohat's place gave rise in me to thoughts of murder. Sometimes I glimpsed one of his patients going in and prostrating themselves in front of him. I was tortured with the desire to tell these simpletons everything I thought, everything I knew. But what was the use? Faith perhaps was sufficient for their well-being. And I sometimes envied them, as one might envy the sleeper who will not be awakened by the fire.

The silence and shadowiness of the place enchanted me despite myself. I fell victim to the charm of the reflections from the stained-glass windows, of the draperies, and the perfumes. Perhaps I, too, would have ended up going down on my knees in the midst of the whisperings and grimaces. But I had only to think for one second of the man of straw behind this charade, and to recall his scared face when I merely raised my voice, to see it all as it really was: a gigantic imposture, a huge farce. Yet, for me, any hope of finding out Dr Fohat's address resided here, and nowhere else. And my confidence in some stroke of good luck led me to push open the front door every day, as meek as I was on the first day, although filled with increasingly violent sarcasm. I must have been regarded as a madman, with the same question constantly on my lips. But what did I care about appearing crazy in the eyes of these menials!

One evening when waves of despondency washed over me, a phrase stole into me like an obsessive refrain. It was as if someone kept coming to whisper in my ear at regular intervals. 'Nothing ends,' was the phrase, 'nothing ends, nothing ends . . .' Unable to escape these two words, I let my thoughts adapt to their rhythm. Nothing ends. You may inadvertently stray from the course mapped out in advance, but the ground covered before straying will not have been a wasted journey. Nothing eliminates the goal, once pursuit of it has begun . . . Nothing ends . . . And suddenly I realized where that phrase came from. It had taken a long time to make its way through who knows what inaccessible country. And now I had a clear perception of it, with the pitch and tone of voice, cloak of silence and context of time and space, even the setting in which it had been uttered. As I came out of Andco & Co. on the morning of my departure, the company's oldest employee had remarked to me, 'Have you noticed that nothing ends?'

Only today did I understand the profound significance of those words. There was not a syllable in the world, not a gesture, that did not have its repercussion somewhere, one day or another. It is terrifying to think that every word we write will be repeated back to us by an inhabitant of interplanetary space, perhaps a few seconds after our death, with the dust of centuries already settled on it. Everything had to be allowed time for its accomplishment, before the sign of it, however humble that sign might be, was dismissed. I walked aimlessly under the trees in the avenue, unable to make up my mind to return to my familiar prison. There were areas of darkness where my face effortlessly resumed the shape of anxiety, its skin clinging to that form exactly like a damp cloth to an old mould. But crossing through each pool of light, the expression I had trained to play its part well reasserted itself, inflating my slack features with a little vital pride. Before passers-by of supposedly my own like, although patently still able to enjoy themselves and laugh at their own fabrications, I could not but feel ashamed of a despair for which there was no good earthly reason. The lights went out one by one. Although I kept pacing the pavement right outside the door to my lodgings, my meditations cast such a new light on everything that I thought I was now wandering in a part of the avenue completely unfamiliar to me. I did not feel sleepy and the night was soon going to be over.

Under the eaves of the roofs, the dawn bats were busy trying to distinguish darkness from daylight. I set off again, automatically following the same direction I took every morning. And I soon saw the sign I knew so well: EYE SPECIALIST.

'What madness,' I thought, 'to come this way! It's beyond question that the doors will be closed at this hour and I'll have to come home dejected.'

Nevertheless, I went on, like the lover who turns

up for his assignation several hours early, in the hope, at the back of his mind, the very small hope, that his beloved will be there, hours early. I pushed against the door, despondent in spirit, already on the point of turning back, when I felt it yield to my pressure and open.

Filled with renewed impatience, I crossed the deserted entrance hall and lobby. The employees had become so indifferent to me, I was not disconcerted by their absence. On the contrary, I was going to be free to shout the question burning on my lips, sure that no one would be able to answer it. With what bitter joy I could then hurl against these impassive walls the blasphemy that would release me from any expectations! And that would be the end of it, at last. Never again would I set foot in this fraudulent place.

However, a slight sound from the ophthalmologist's office made me continue my investigations in silence. Entering that room for the second time, I thought it seemed brighter, more intimate, more spacious than on the day I gave a drubbing to Dr Fohat's successor. Bundles of paper spilled out of drawers as if the occupant of the office had surprisedly been compelled to leave it. I thought I could even detect an invisible presence, and my heart began to pound dizzyingly. And indeed, all at once, I saw that I was not alone.

There was an old woman at my feet, looking up at me. She had a bucket of dirty water beside her, and her fingers were wringing out a floor-cloth over it. She stopped what she was doing when saw me come in. She was a very poor old woman. Her clothes blended into the gloom and her wrinkled hands were the colour of the cloth they were squeezing. But there was such profound submission in her colourless eyes, I immediately felt overwhelmed with an abundant pity before them. And I fell at this woman's knees, and took the dripping cloth from her worn hands. Forgotten was the question that had been torturing me night after night. But I did not need to say a word. Because she was able to relieve my distress. She alone knew the cause of it.

'Yes, yes,' she murmured in a voice I shall never forget, 'I know where Dr Fohat lives . . .'

That same evening the passers-by who recognized me, standing amid the mob of underlings blocking the pavement, looked back, astounded. But imagine their amazement, when the old charlady appeared, at seeing me offer her my arm with every sign of respect and affection. Her colleagues, who were in the habit of superciliously walking past her without even saying goodbye, losing no opportunity to jostle her a bit as a clear sign of their superiority, stood there flabbergasted and laughed coarsely, the low esteem they had for me turning to triumphant disdain. But what did I care about their foolish insolence? This old woman in her isolation and poverty was dearer to me than any of them. And so we made our way to the restaurant that I had gone into the first evening, I, defying the multitude, and she, filled with secret pride. There, again, we had to endure the onslaught of people's stares and soon the menacing swell of sniggering and murmuring.

'Yes, he has lovely eyes,' people said, 'but he's blind!'

Women pale with jealousy did not demur at expressing their opinion aloud. I remained silent, knowing the word that would have crushed them all. Yet, shame such as I had never before experienced constricted my throat. But it was shame for this crowd, for its meanness, its suddenly displayed, unrestrained vulgarity. My companion gazed at me, only at me, with those eyes worn out by sleepless nights, in which resignation had given way to a subdued, as it were veiled, pride. She seemed to be wondering with surprising confidence how far my patience would extend. Oh, I was so happy and she could understand why! I wished that the unshakeable certainty of my being different might engrave itself on her soul. With no need for words, my presence beside her clearly conveyed the message: I am not one of them. I only came to live on the avenue by accident, as you well know. Why do you still seem to doubt it? But a little mischievousness deep in her eyes told me she no longer doubted it, that in the face of my lofty silence she could no longer have any doubt. And my earlier scorn for those around us turned to serene indulgence, akin almost to tenderer feelings. I wished that moment might never end! At the end of the meal, we left together, through the small door. The deserted streets were blanched with moonlight.

'My friend,' she said, 'you have a long walk ahead of you. But now I know you have the courage for it.'

I could tell that her heart was full of regret, which she tried hard not to show. Sensing we were soon going to part, she whispered some words that might have seemed inconsequential to anyone else, but which I understood as if they had been inscribed in fulminant letters on the black screen of darkness.

'Farewell,' I said abruptly, so that the emotion which, from the trembling of our hands, I felt was increasing, should calm down in solitude.

And when I turned round to give her a final wave, her tottering figure was already being swallowed up by the night.

I had a moment's hesitation before the entranceway. An icy fog, bringing sounds closer, made the discordant cries of a depressing world rattle in my ears. I had walked all night long through dead streets. And morning found me far from my destination. Now I was so weary I almost regretted my cosy room, at this time of day when the avenue began to grow animated with the bustle of its happy strollers. To add to my distress, I could not find, among the multitude of plaques giving the names of tenants, the square of paper saying what floor Dr Fohat was on. I thought the wind and bad weather must have long since destroyed it, and that he, being no ordinary businessman, had no doubt failed to replace it. I recognized the damp courtyard with the open staircase at the back of it, and entered, my heart beating with emotion in a new and fervent impatience. At last I reached the fourth floor. The door had been repainted, but standing out clearly on the begrimed, rough-plastered wall was the place where the old plaque had been. There was no bell any more (I was certainly the last to pull it, so infelicitously!). I knocked on this unfamiliar door and immediately heard, from behind it, voices and hurried footsteps. A woman who looked like a bawd opened the door.

'Come in, monsieur . . .' she said.

But I realized straightaway there was some mistake. A curtain hung over a second doorway and through the opening I glimpsed a bar counter on which a young woman was leaning on her elbows. With her every gesture, her brown locks of hair moved on her dazzlingly white, bare back, and I heard stifled voices and giggles nearby. I hesitated for another interminable moment, during which the temptation came over me, as in a flash, to cast aside the memory of Dr Fohat for ever, and abandon the purpose of my visit. Then I explained to the woman who had come to the door that I wanted to see the ophthalmologist who used to live in this apartment. The moment she knew what I wanted, she disappeared. But she soon returned, accompanied by a dozen creatures, some wearing wraps, others who had not even the basic courtesy to don that scant attire. They were all laughing hysterically and some kept repeating inanely, 'Dr Fohat . . . Dr Fohat . . .'

I was waiting for them to explain what was so terribly funny about my plight, when one of them, suddenly raising the pitch of her voice several degrees, began to shout, 'Dr Fohat . . . Dr Fohat!'

And the whole lot of them laughed all the more, some with an atrocious laughter like the cry of guinea fowl. The door was still open and, at the noise these women were making, there soon appeared from every floor all kinds of people who seemed to have just got out of bed, although it was now the middle of the day. Those who were not in night-shirts had hastily thrown on some old jacket, pyjamas, or other togs for wearing round the house. There were even some completely naked. There was something frightful and grotesque, like a bad joke from the mouth of a dying man, about the sight of this braying herd – for all of them, as soon as they realized what was going on, began to chant the same refrain as these ladies. Now they accompanied their cries with a gesture that consisted of pointing a finger in the air with their arms raised. This dance of savages brought my rage to the boil. I was about to explode when suddenly I had an intuition that by gesticulating in this way they were indicating to me the upper floors. Then, jostling several of the females who were clutching at my clothes, I went racing up the stairs and soon that squawking was no more than a distant murmur behind me.

I would never have believed there could be so many floors in that building. I arrived, short of breath, under the eaves. A strange calm came over me. A soft glow from a fanlight filled the dusty-walled corridor. At the end of this corridor, on the ill-joined battens of a door, were chalked the simple words: ALEXANDRE FOHAT. Here, in this attic, lived the man whose memory had haunted me

for years. I suddenly noticed the underlying harmony uniting certain categories of things. The floor-
cleaner's gaze was like these bare planks of wood,
this chalked notice, their poverty full of a mysterious, intangible wealth. Casting my mind even further back, I recalled the place where I had survived
on the intake of only one tablet a day. In that ascet-
icism, that detachment, resided my truth. But then,
everything was as though tainted with immorality.
Base individuals, base thoughts always tarnished my
quest. The same desire for a cure quivered inside
me, here and now, stronger and more sincere because
in the meantime I had had experience of everything but this desire, this pursuit – and nothing had
brought me contentment. I took a few steps towards
the door and felt as if I were on a road cleansed by
darkness, when day is about to break. Several metres
separated me still from the wooden partition when
it slowly opened. Dr Fohat came towards me, with
his hands outstretched. All he uttered was my
name. But that was enough to lift my soul like a
wave that carries you far from the shore, for ever. I
had completely forgotten why I came. I had nothing
to say any more; there was nothing left to say. An
unconcerned bather swimming out to sea watched by
unconcerned onlookers on the shore.

A large wooden table and two chairs constituted
the basic furnishings of this eyrie. The only decor-
ation on the whitewashed walls was a glass showcase
behind which I thought I glimpsed a collection of
insects. But although my gaze was attracted by this
showcase, to tell the truth I could not make out

clearly what was in it. The pathetic cooing of doves nesting under the roof, or the sudden flurry of a bird taking flight, could be heard from time to time. Dr Fohat sat down in the chair that remained unoccupied, and the huge, empty table separated us. He seemed immersed in contemplation of his nervous hands. Then he lifted his face and I saw that his features had undergone a change, and were no longer the same as before. How wrong I was to have taken him for an old man!

'I knew you would come back to see me, Marcel Adrien,' he began. 'All those who have once consulted me cannot but return. But as far as you're concerned, there must be some mistake. The ailments from which you suffer, I cannot cure. I'm not a doctor, nor do I sell spectacles. In the past, I did for a while practise the honourable profession of ophthalmologist . . . But you yourself knew at the time all that was just a game . . . It's insofar as this was not unknown to you that your case, among so many others, interests me. A great confusion continues still to exist in our relationship. But be fair and trusting – fair and trusting, exactly that – and you'll see that everything will soon become clear between us . . .'

As he spoke, his hands moved across the table in a broad gesture, as though to sweep the surface of it, then he leaned back, and the penetrating gaze he had kept fixed on me became lost as it shifted to the large windows.

'Do you yearn for better eyesight,' he went on, 'to the point of sacrificing everything else? Or is not

your objective rather the need to reconcile the con-
flicting forces warring inside you? I know the language I'm speaking is obscure. I know I'm brandish-
ing phrases in front of you like mirrors: the sun often
comes and blurs the reflection that would appear
in them. If I could express what I have to say in
some other way, I wouldn't use ambiguous language.
Moreover, I've no key for those who find my message
impenetrable. All I ask of them, as I do of you, is to
be fair and trusting. You see how the tone of my
words has already changed since the first day you
appeared before me. And yet you're listening to me.
I'm not so remote that you can't hear me, that you
even have any desire to stop hearing me. And all this
way you've come without me has not put any distance between us. That's the real miracle! If you
continue to follow me, even without seeming to, even
just pretending to, together we'll reach our objective.
Fortunately,' he continued, 'I didn't have to try out
on myself every one of my discoveries. My patients
are so numerous that my testing ground was always, so to speak, unlimited. Many will tell you that
they've been cured by me. Well, let me tell you: the
eyesight of a blind person who thinks he sees well
never gets any better. Cured? They were no more
cured than you are. What I gave them all was a different opportunity, since they were each the subject
of a different experiment. Most of the time the result
was not what my patient reckoned on. But I want
you to understand: I was the only person who knew
what the result should be. They all helped me in my
research. They all contributed to achieving my goal.

That was the only thing that really mattered, and it was of very little importance whether or not I could explain it to them.

'Most men don't see because they're all too accustomed to seeing. Treating the eye, correcting vision . . . the unrealistic aspiration of dull-witted pedants, who confuse cause with effect. You have to shift the gaze, change the angle of vision so that the essential truth appears in new relief. Tailor each person's way of looking to suit his capacity, since it's impossible to tailor the world to suit everyone's way of looking.'

These confidences held me breathless despite myself. They were imparted in a tone of total detachment, but one that occasionally became suddenly insinuating, urgent, as though to appeal to my instinctive understanding rather than my reason. I was intrigued, bewildered by this extraordinary character, but at the same time vaguely disturbed. He lowered his eyes only to take furtive looks at my face, and these rapid glances filled me with a disquiet akin to fear. 'What was he driving at?' I could not help wondering. Luckily, I had my back to the windows, and while the light fell strongly on his face, my features were cast in shadow. I felt a little reassured by the fact that he could not see from my expression my reactions to his words.

'Spectacles,' he went on, 'are a wonderful invention, but a poet's invention, an illusionist's invention. I think I've pursued to their worst conclusions the consequences of this discovery, whose normal and practical use – to relieve eye-strain – is all that most of my colleagues know about it. You're already familiar with sleep-inducing spectacles?'

At these words, I saw the smile of old return to his face for a brief moment, the smile that had seemed to me indelible. And I realized in what way his appearance had changed: an anxious reserve, similar to the deep gravity of despair, had replaced that former smile.

'I succeeded in making the antidote: spectacles to prevent sleep. My research into the properties of certain transparent materials led me, always for recreation, to create spectacles for every need, for every eventuality: spectacles to counter anger, idleness, envy. My patients could obtain from my shops, at their choice, aphrodisiac spectacles or ones that cure love; spectacles made of alectorian stone that cancel the harmful effect of poisons, others made of chrysoprase that have the gift of strengthening weakened wills; spectacles that procure a grandiose, thrilling idea of the world, or ones that reduce it to the dimensions of a reading room . . . ones that give a blue view of life or a rose-tinted view; spectacles that induce dreams or suppress them . . . in a word, the most fantastic assortment of spectacles imaginable.

'But, as you can well understand, they were only spectacles – for fun, I mean. You only had to take them off and their power immediately ceased to be effective. Whoever bought any – and you weren't meant to choose more than one pair, because one cancelled the power of another – couldn't rivet this fragile instrument to his flesh. Sooner or later, he'd have to take them off and become himself again: a poor fellow only beguiled by this temporary illusion. I'm not talking about accidentally breaking them, which would plunge the bereft owner into despair or incapability . . .

'I conceived of the idea of a medication combining certain vision-fortifiers with certain psychic elements that would enhance their properties. The great difficulty was working out the doses of this regimen, to curb its virulence and protect the organism from its noxiousness. I managed to do this by counterbalancing its effects with a lapse of time between each dose, during which the patient should at no point remain inactive. Unfortunately, the treatment took many years and this slowness often discouraged my patients. Besides, the manufacture of the pills was so tricky, it required the never-failing reliability of a large staff. To this end, I set up the Fohat Company, a veritable factory, comprising an entire neighbourhood of old buildings in which my workers were accommodated. But the distribution of these pills needed to be secured, and I had to acquire, in addition, huge stores on the main avenue of a smart neighbourhood, as far away as possible from the production centre. At the head of this enterprise, I soon found myself beset with problems that had no connection with my previous work. Between the square, where the factory was located, and the avenue, where the sales were made, there was a perpetual coming and going, which I had constantly to supervise. When I became aware of the dispersion, the lack of concentration occasioned by these multiple activities, despite the funds and time I had already sunk into this venture, I sold the firm off to some real businessmen, with no knowledge at all of its objectives but with the qualities necessary for its prosperity. The Alexandre Fohat Company became Andco & Co., and my shop on the avenue changed ownership.'

At that point the doctor rose and went over to the glass case that had attracted my attention earlier. I followed him. Laid out in rows on narrow shelves were some egg-sized balls, with a peculiarly iridescent surface.

'Do you know what these are? They're eyes! Yes, eyes. They're not yet in their final form, but look at those ones, which are finished.'

So saying, he pointed out to me, on one of the other shelves, six pairs of eyes, whose resemblance to real eyes was absolutely unnerving.

'In short, all my past experiments led me to this conclusion: why make spectacles or pills to improve eyesight, when it's so simple to manufacture eyes? Today, I don't sell glasses any more, I sell eyes. My patients are not as numerous as before! The moment one does anything out of the ordinary, people become wary. Total novelty frightens them. I admit my idea might seem daring. But while imagination is the tissue with which an inventor creates a world, he will never succeed without daring, his only tool. Anyway, I'm not sorry that my patient list has thinned out. I have no great needs and my few remaining patients will always be enough to keep me going. Only a very small number of exceptional individuals, 'adventurers' if I may give that word its full meaning, consent with the necessary trust to the operation I indicate to them. To take a new chance and run the risk of losing every alternative does indeed call for singular courage.'

At the very moment of uttering these words, Dr Fohat looked at me. And it was as if, having so far mistaken me for someone else, a stranger, he recognized me, accepted me as one of his own caste, a fellow countryman, a member of his family. He took hold of my hands and I felt quivers running through his.

'What was just a game before,' he went on, 'a game that we played with the utmost seriousness, today becomes very solemn, involving your life and my earlier experiments. No evasion, no compromise, no alternative is possible any more. If you accept what I'm proposing, your entire past will acquire a meaning, everything that should have been your downfall will contribute to your salvation. Yet, you have to understand that you'll lose everything else but your gaze. The operation is not without risk. It sometimes confers on the person who undergoes it a strange and dangerous power that even I know nothing about ... But you should also understand that no man will have ever had clearer vision than yours. You have to choose: on the one hand, the dimness through which you stumbled here, and on the other hand, unfettered, airy light ... In exchange, you have to run this risk, take this possibly terrible chance ...'

I must have listened to this speech – the glib soliloquy of a mythomane, or dry report of a technical expert? – in a kind of stupefaction. Luckily, a small incident occurred at that moment to break the tension of our conversation. There were several knocks at the door.

'Come in!' said Dr Fohat in a completely changed voice, in which I thought I detected a slight weariness.

I did not expect to see an angel appear. And surely the old woman who came gliding in, in her slippers, without looking at us, and set down on the table a loaf of bread and a jug of milk, was the only angel with access to this place? But her silent intervention at least gave me the assurance that the terms in which her master spoke were not as insubstantial as I tended to believe.

'Your eyes are splendid,' he resumed after this brief interruption, 'I've never seen such beautiful eyes in my entire career! Ah, my treatment would have achieved wonders in that respect!'

He seemed to dream for a moment, then suddenly went on, 'But it's not a question of having beautiful eyes. However splendid they might be, I must replace those eyes of yours with eyes of my own invention.'

He came towards me as he spoke, and held me with his gaze. How can such moments be described? I was divided between the dread of suffering and the desire to gratify the will of this magician. The thought of challenging his words never even crossed my mind, but a secret anxiety made me stave off their accomplishment. Would not the scene that must follow resemble those awful moments before waking up in a sweat? I resisted it, saying over and over again, 'I'm not dreaming . . . I'm not dreaming . . . But if the truth was that it did have to happen, then at least let there be no waking up, that it should not have happened in vain! And it was the certainty of not being in a dream that made me accept the worst with inhuman serenity. Dr Fohat's gaze was like a refuge I felt myself slipping towards, while at the same time spurning it. For a long time, since his first words, I had been nothing but a small child in his hands, a small child who both fears and welcomes the salutary operation. I would have suffered a thousand deaths sooner than disobey him. Then, in the midst of the perturbation that was raising great walls of mist around me, I saw the doctor draw a steel instrument from his pockets. Those pincers, shining like suns, grew inordinately large in my field of vision. Then there was darkness. I suffered no pain, barely feeling the cold caress of metal on the edge of my eyelids. When I regained consciousness, I saw my eyes, my old eyes, resting on the table.

THE STUDIO

Just as passion alone changes people, so too fire alone transforms matter, constituent of form. What it devours only increases its voraciousness. It is the grand master of phantasmagorias, the preferred element of monsters. Beneath its manic robes, the steps of its rumba combine with the capers of the ancient dance of death. Fire blackens but purifies what it touches. When everything is consumed, its extinction is sometimes daintily adorned with white-ash lacing.

A moving mist like a curtain of hot air came between me and everything else. Dr Fohat led me to the door, which I would not have found without his help.

'Don't worry, a few minutes' patience behind that veil . . . and you'll be cured.'

He had scarcely uttered these words when I felt as though I had been cut off from his presence. Alone in a hostile world, I opted to close my eyes and, feeling my way along the wall, I headed for the top of the stairs. It was better to stumble through the shadows towards daylight, than to run blithely in the light towards darkness. Though my eyes had forgotten the narrow corridor under the eaves, my feet, hands, and memory recognized it. I descended several storeys, umpteen storeys. It was like descending the spiral staircase of a high tower. The number of steps between each floor being always the same, and the width of each landing recurring with perfect regularity, my legs, getting used to this rhythm, soon continued to work automatically. My descent became faster and faster, speeded along by this untiring mechanism. I was almost dancing as I blindly flew down, finally propelled, by the momentum I gained, back to the ground floor at last.

I opened my eyes. The moving curtain was gone; everything had regained its distinctness and customary immobility. But I did not recognize the court-yard. Yet it was certainly the same place, although everything in it was, to my eyes, transformed. Surfaces were surrounded by a halo of varying widths, sometimes reduced to a slender glittering border. This pale, diversely tinted brightness outlined every recess, every overhanging stone, every ledge. A small statue, in a niche above a door, floated in a thick red band. The very paving stones were as though set in dark opal. My new eyes, with their capacity to see even the irradiation of matter, put me at the centre of a marvellous world whose existence I could not have suspected before. Slowly, I crossed the court-yard, without tiring of looking and trying, in my rapture, to analyse my impressions. Something oppressed me, perhaps regret at having left Dr Fohat so suddenly, perhaps too a vague nostalgia for the old world I had just lost for ever. I was overwhelmed by a sudden feeling of loneliness. How can I convey what was henceforth to be my daily lot? In the corner of the doorway, a fat woman sitting on a bollard stared at me. Her face, haloed with pearly grey, had the blackish pink tinge of new-born babies. As I was passing her, I saw a greenish lizard emerge from her mouth and scuttle inside her smock.

A certain distance, a slight remove, I soon noticed, were needed to preserve the miracle. As soon as I went to touch the object that attracted my curiosity, it regained its former character. I realized this, I have to admit, with a kind of relief. Nevertheless, I advanced cautiously along the walls, not taking the risk of letting my gaze linger on passers-by. Before daring to look at people (everyone brushing past was like a universe that would easily have drawn me into its orb), I had to get used to the setting in which they moved. Sometimes I hesitated to step on certain bits of the pavement for fear they were alive. Seeing some shiny thing gleaming in the gutter, I bent down and reached for it: it was just a rotten fruit that had been thrown away.

Everything, at every moment, filled me with wonder and amazement, and but for the phenomenon whereby my old perception of surrounding objects kept being restored to me, just in time, I would never have been able to get used to steering my way through this fairyland. The houses, the street and the vehicles congesting it, the tide of passers-by appeared to be streaming with water wrested from luminous depths. All these shimmerings took nothing away of the precision of detail, but on the contrary showed up their superimposition and relief, imparting to images an unexpected perspective of extraordinary clarity. Words float like thick veils round my vision, distorting it more than revealing it. Any man with normal eyesight – I mean, more or less affected with myopia, as I had once been – will be hard put to imagine the multiplicity of my feelings. There is perhaps nothing to equal clear-sightedness. The hereditary notion of values that makes us bestow greater importance on a rare object, or misleads our senses in front of what we are accustomed to calling 'beauty', was annulled within me. Every item, every creature, divested of its conventional relations with the rest of the world, was isolated, suspended in its true place, wearing the sacred seal of its own existence. Everything had to be separated before the secret link between the humblest and grandest things became apparent to me.

Filled with enthusiasm, as though walking in my sleep, I must have reached the edge of town. Everything was so wonderfully beautiful to my eyes that I did not feel tired. Through wide-open windows and doors, I glimpsed families gathered round for supper in the soft dusk before the lights are turned on. Without the least desire to sit down at one of these tables, I blessed Dr Fohat for having given me a different perception of things.

At sunset I was still walking, along a road bordered with trees where the last suburban houses became fewer and far between. Evening had diminished and, as it were, blurred the luminous contour of things, or perhaps it was only their lesser diversity that gave me this impression. I was in the throes of ecstasy, and it did not occur to me to check closely the true aspect of my surroundings. I was still under the spell cast over me by the revelation of the outside world. Maybe that evening was just like any other evening, but the day had been so full, so new, that the breeze in the trees added further to my enchantment and I thought, as I listened to it, that I detected an ineffable singing. I saw the rising moon as an extraordinary star as incomprehensible to me as the rotten fruit in the gutter. In this ravishment, I could only wonder by what inconceivable grace I had the privilege of belonging to this wondrous universe. And I fell asleep in the hollow of an embankment with nothing to detract from my contentment.

Ah! How terrible that day's ransom was to appear to me the next day! The morning coolness woke me, and at once an immense joy swept over me, at the certainty of still being alive, of still participating in the same enchantment as I had experienced the previous day.

'All my awakenings will be like this from now on . . .' I said to myself, so swiftly does the spirit get used to what convulses it.

A pink mist floated over the countryside, suspended from roofs, clinging to fences, and every little leaf of every tree glistened like a fish in water. I headed towards a bell-tower, an arrow of flame in the distance. I saw each blade of grass at the roadside emerge from sleep and stretch with contentment in the dew's embrace. I saw each flower open to behold the day. I was that flower, that blade of grass, that bell-tower on the horizon. My feet scarcely touched the road and my head sailed along, up in the sky, like a ship breasting a wave of crystal clarity. Beyond this transparency, the countryside looked to me like a scene located several kilometres away, but foreshortened, inordinately enlarged by translucent depths. Soon new dwellings appeared in this scene and it seemed astonishing to me that I could touch their walls by simply stretching out my hand.

'All this exists, all this exists!' I said to myself again and again. 'And I never saw it before!'

I realized what blindness I had suffered, and I could not believe that my recovery was so complete.

Sudden awareness of the independent life of things gave me insight into their mutual relations, which were not, as I had previously thought, all a matter of chaos and anarchy. A luminous order prevailed over this arrangement, was the cement uniting each of its elements. And I saw and understood this, and there was no room for any doubt. The certainty that came from my new gaze was very like an intoxication: I was reeling as I entered the low-ceilinged room of an inn.

All the magnificence of the world notwithstanding, the thought of refreshment had finally occurred to me. In the gloom, objects and furniture cast a diffuse light. I sat at a table whose worn surface was like old velvet. A young waitress appeared and – as if I were seeing a human face for the first time – I dared to raise my eyes and look at her. Bedazzlement! While objects were as though imprisoned by their halo, the flesh of this face palpitated in the midst of its own light, glittered like an iridescent flame. I tried to contain my emotion so as to order a snack from this girl. I was eager to be alone again, to sort out my impressions. When she had set down the frugal meal, and a knife and fork, in front of me, I felt relieved to see her go. But my attention was immediately drawn to the objects still quivering from her touch. They seemed to waver above the table, within reach of my hand.

Now, how can I possibly describe what happened next, without taxing the reader's credulity? I was about to take hold of the knife in order to use it, that knife gleaming on the velvet table, isolated from the

rest of the world by a yellow outline. But hardly had
my fingers lightly closed round the handle when it
silently shattered in my hand and was reduced to
dust. Fear, a terrible fear, at once brought a rush of
blood to my cheeks. With the eyes of a hunted beast
I looked to see if anyone had witnessed the astound-
ing phenomenon produced by mere contact with my
hand. No, I was quite alone. Then I picked up the
fork, thinking I must have been the victim of an
illusion. But the same thing happened again: I felt
the metal crumble between my fingers, disintegrate
as if it were nothing but a cluster of unsubstantial
molecules.

Thereupon, I recalled Dr Fohat's words: 'You'll
lose everything else but your gaze . . . In exchange,
in compensation, a strange and dangerous power
will be conferred on you – what power, even I don't
know . . .' Peculiar light was thrown on other
phrases: 'Everything becomes very solemn today . . .
You have to run a risk . . . this possibly terrible
chance . . .'

Everything I had taken for symbolic wording was
literal truth. No retreat was possible. Once again the
evidence of that fact was crushing: since the very
first day, since that distant day when I entered Dr
Fohat's surgery, no retreat had been possible. I had
to accept my law and come to terms with it, on my
own. I was trembling in every limb, imploring heaven
that no one should enter the room at that moment.
Bent over my plate, I managed to consume its contents without the aid of my fingers, the way a dog
laps up its food. And I made my escape, to hide my

dismay out on the road that was luckily still deserted.

For how long did I hurry away like a madman? Far from any habitation, I finally dropped to the ground, staring stupidly at a stone at my feet. Slowly, carefully, I reached towards it. And I managed, almost without touching it, to roll it in the hollow of my hand. The hope that a momentary aberration had led my senses to blunder a short while ago prevented me from closing my fingers round this smooth, white stone whose astonishing lightness I experienced with delight. I finally put myself to the test. The stone immediately burst like a bubble. Nothing was left in my palm but a dark dust blown away by the wind. I stared at my empty hand, appalled.

Would it be possible to survive, if I took infinite precautions? Knowing at what degree of pressure the dissolving power of my touch came into effect, could I perhaps succeed in mastering it? Without entirely dispelling my anxiety, this idea gave me a little comfort. For a moment my confidence returned, and I allowed myself to be reconquered by the surrounding beauty. Everything claimed my attention, as though encouraging me to forget the jinx upon me. But the temptation to control its effects suddenly came over me again. A branch I picked up shattered to bits as soon as my fingers took hold of it. With anxious feverishness I repeated the experiment several times. I had to master this terrible power, to discipline it. Doubtless I would only succeed in doing so in solitude, through patience. I would have to reduce my touch to the lightest of grazes, and avoid seizing too avidly what was offered to me to take. It was a total training of my senses that I would have to undergo, a new preparation for life. Scared at having become so different from other people, I could not without shuddering envisage the ostracization that would accompany me everywhere, like a curse. Revelation of this pernicious power was the revelation of a danger. It excluded me in advance from the human community, and despite myself my thoughts were already those of a pariah.

At that moment I saw, approaching, two young people of great beauty – or so it appeared to me. What did these newcomers, intruding on my field of vision, want of me? Like the waitress at the inn, they radiated such brilliance it was hard to look at them. They took up the whole width of the road, as they walked along, each carrying the handle of a large basket that swung between them in rhythm with their step. The face of one reflected energy and goodness, while grace and nobility were to be read in the features of the other. Coming to halt several paces away, they greeted me, having set their basket down on the ground. It was full of terracotta figurines representing a great variety of subjects. I was then seized with the desire to astound these two lads. I reached out for their wares and carefully managed to pick up one of the statuettes, a small naked child raising a bunch of grapes above his smiling lips. When it was right under the noses of these two silent pedlars, I suddenly squeezed my fingers and it shattered into a thousand minute particles, like a dried mushroom ground to dust under the heel of a boot. I had imagined the amazement that was going to appear on the two young men's faces. To my great surprise, they merely looked at me with pity, which did not fail to rouse a dull anger in me. I was going to do the same thing again. But without a word, one of them caught me by the wrist, while the other took hold of the little statue that I was going to grab, and lifted it up before my eyes. It was a tiny dancer with finely modelled legs that looked as if they were just about to come to life. There was so much elegance and awkwardness in her pose, such vitality and beauty that I immediately regretted the act I had intended to commit, as if it had been murder. And I realized once again that my power was a baleful one. Out of pity for myself, I began to weep profusely, in all my remorse and shame.

When I looked up again, I was sitting in the grass on the embankment, and the two young men were standing on either side of me, trying to console me with many wordless demonstrations of affection. Their silent presence calmed me in my distress. At that moment I could not have tolerated for one second the sound of a human voice. They seemed unconcerned about their basket now, being solely absorbed by the desire to please me. When I realized they understood my language, I told them my story, going back to my first interview with Dr Fohat. After a long pause, in which they appeared to consult each other with the aid of signs agreed between them, the one whose manliness of face had impressed me drew from his pocket a sheet of paper and scribbled on it for a while, then handed it to me.

I learnt by this means that his name was Fulbert and his friend was called Eudes. While both were stricken with dumbness, this infirmity did not prevent them from hearing. Neither one nor the other had ever sought out a doctor to cure them. They even seemed to be of the same mind in doubting the existence of such a possibility, and they were not at all bothered by this. They had eventually found comfort for their misfortunes in the practice of their profession. Eudes was the artist who made the figurines, while Fulbert was responsible for selling them. The note added that, right now, the two companions were on their way to town, but my story and something about me had both touched and enchanted them. They suggested staying with me, if I had no objection. Their presence would certainly be of valuable assistance. The tokens of affection shown by these two tall youths prompted me to accept their proposal straight away. They knew that my footsteps were aimless when they encountered me, and that their destination was to become my own. We sealed this extraordinary pact between the three of us with long and careful hugs.

Some time later, I was on the road, following these two mute brothers with their swinging basket, who had just rescued me from a solitariness that would surely have been the death of me. Yet they had not deprived me of its essential magic. The sound that their shoes made gave me somewhat the impression of the double echo of my own footsteps.

As time went by, this impression grew stronger. Soon it seemed to me that all the conversational remarks, reproaches, or confidences I might wish to make to these two friends were directed not so much to them as to myself. At first, our life was perfectly organized. They were lavish in their care for me, and always on the watch for my least gesture. Very quickly, with the sole object of averting any repetition of distressing accidents in the presence of others, they conspired not to leave anything within my reach, going so far as to help me take my meals without the need to use my fingers. For my part, I was also very useful to them, simply by virtue of having the invaluable advantage of speech. In short, we complemented each other: I gave them the convenience of speech and they gave me the benefit of touch without danger. My eyesight alone retained its independence and it sometimes pained me that for them everything was dull and joyless, whereas I had regained in their company the privilege and possibility of living in wonderment.

We were so tired on reaching town, on the evening of the day we met, that we decided to rest on a bench in a public garden. One of those little gardens where every day the dreams of a hundred citizens take flight, from the unblemished tips of its leaves. The next day, Fulbert, who was definitely the brightest of the three of us, went to enquire about somewhere to stay. He eventually discovered, in the narrow street of a deserted neighbourhood, a place that included a shop for unspecified use. There was no doubt that sales of the figurines would prosper here.

As for myself, where I lived, the choice of a neigh-bourhood or of lodgings, and all other contingencies of the kind that had once been of great concern to me, had become a matter of total indifference. My life, wherever it was spent, was now unassailable. At least, that is what I thought. Dr Fohat's operation, by making clearly perceptible what my eyes would never have been able even to glimpse before, put ugliness, together with beauty, on a new plane, so that they became confused. I felt the same emotional shock in front of both. I was surprised before each thing. Without, however, losing its essential char-acter, everything I saw was transformed, as if beneath unexpected lighting, by its halo, its bril-liance, by a new perspective. Filth and rags became scenery as interesting as neatness and elegance; a dilapidated wall, the window of a hovel, or the most squalid street had the same attraction – although different – as the most modern building, the most expensive boulevard. Wherever the eye rests, it embraces all the mystery of the world. It would have cost me the effort of only a few steps to return to those places familiar to my memories, but I did not think of doing so. Like Edith's death, Dr Fohat's operation had opened a new era in my life, had brought me to a new summit: the crest of a wave, down which I had only to let myself slide, to where the trough is darkest, before being caught again in another upflow that would lift me yet higher, to where the foam is whitest.

Eudes and I spent our days in a room attached to the

shop that served us as a studio. A grille was fitted, through which I could speak to clients, while Fulbert, behind a counter, showed them the figurines, his pleasing looks having conferred this role on him. He was there to receive potential buyers, I to translate his gestures into words and to give prices. Eudes was the only one who did not take part in these transactions. He would not have been capable of it. He spent his whole time making new items. But while Fulbert and I cooperated in selling, my collaboration with Eudes was no less important.

From the very outset I noticed that customers had little enthusiasm for his statuettes. These figurines were too much like the ones you could buy for a few coins on market stalls or in junk shops. It was just my eyesight that so transformed these humble artefacts that I took them for real works of art. Ah, if only Eudes could see things as I did! Surely his creations would have the brilliancy of masterpieces! I had the idea of helping him with my advice, of instilling him, as it were, with my own vision. The most difficult thing was to persuade him. But when he realized that I would allow him total freedom in the execution of the figurines and that he would continue, as in the past, to sign them solely with his name, he accepted my proposal.

We were swiftly rewarded for our efforts. Buyers came flocking when new models, made according to my suggestions, filled the shelves. So the services my two friends rendered me were amply compensated for by my activity, in every domain. My position at the grille set me astride their respective dependencies on

me: with one foot in each camp. Without leaving
Eudes' studio, I was at the counter with Fulbert. So
I understood every difficulty their jobs entailed,
whereas between them, and though I did everything
I could to avoid it, numerous misunderstandings
became greater every day.

One day, when a young lady customer had just
chosen a little faun, it seemed to me that Fulbert, by
his looks and even his gestures, was singularly
exceeding his duties as a salesman. She was a beautiful red-haired girl, whose seductive voice seemed to
emanate from her very genitals. Like a large fly buzz-
ing round, she disturbed the studio where Eudes was
industriously bent over one of his drawings. Finally,
suspicious of his friend's behaviour, noticing how
long-drawn out the conversation was getting, how
heavy the silences, he could not restrain himself from
rushing into the shop.

'I'm the maker of this masterpiece, not this
jumped-up shopkeeper!' he said to the pretty customer, or rather conveyed to her by means of many
gestures, obliging me to translate those that were not
clear enough.

I watched this ridiculous scene from my grille,
seeking to reconcile the fools, trying by my laconi-
cism to bring an end to their mutual blazing fervour.
There is nothing exaggerated about this description:
these two mutes rampaging round their lovely prey
had an almost scary fascination. The woman's body
flashed all over with an opaque and yellow light, and
my two friends were like grotesque short-winged but-
terflies, diving into this beacon. Objects that already,

under their normal aspect, I did not tire of looking at, took on, from the intensity of feelings emanating from these individuals, a fantastic appearance it is impossible to describe. Fulbert climbed on to the counter to strike the pose, in front of the alluring young lady, of the little faun she was interested in. With her undeniable talent for grasping the meaning of demonstrations of this kind, she immediately understood that if the gentleman artist was the author of the charming object, the gentleman salesman was the model for it.

After she left the premises, accompanied by Fulbert, the winner of the contest, I consoled Eudes. But these sorts of incidents left me, too, dissatisfied. After all, I could have told this lady that without my guidance neither the maker nor the model would have succeeded in creating the little faun that she liked. Above all, I could have expressed my own feelings to her, instead of restricting myself to translating, even while slightly betraying, those of my friends. But true to the pact binding us, I always remained in the background in such circumstances, contenting myself with being a spokesman when I would have had much more to say on my own behalf.

This self-denial was not the least difficult aspect of my role, especially as feelings of desire towards pretty customers became at least as strong in me as in my two accomplices. Incidents pitting Eudes and Fulbert against each other in this way recurred frequently, each time increasing in intensity. The former could not observe the constant success of the latter without resentment turning to acrimony. The presence of Fulbert, who had a very individual way of fixing his powerful gaze on their proud and submissive eyes, attracted all these female creatures like bitches on heat. Our shop soon became a veritable place of assignation and the constant sight of these perfumed and, to my eyes, miraculously beautiful beings robbed me of all peace of mind. What torture having to renounce the thousand desires the sight of them bred in my imagination! Impossible, because of the oppressive jinx on me, to transfer these pressing needs to the level of reality. Even their partial satisfaction would have entailed multiple accidents. And I lived in frustration and sadness. Eudes, consumed with envy, like me, was still able to satisfy himself with second best. Very often, both of them would leave me behind in the empty studio. For a long time I would watch the marvellous effects of the dying light as evening fell. Sometimes, during those moments of loneliness, I could not resist the temptation to exercise the extraordinary power that made me into this eternal recluse. Grabbing one of the little statues within my reach, I would then remain for hours staring at the intangible dust to which it was immediately reduced by my touch. So, I had this power, and because of it I had to live like a pariah, isolated as an undesirable. Oh, how I longed to burst through the doors and go walking through the streets, with my hands open, like weapons! I only resisted the desire out of 'prudence', an elegant euphemism for cowardice. One step outside without the help of my companions would have led to my ruin. The insecurity of my life, of being at the mercy of these two skirt-chasers, was more apparent to me than ever.

It was monstrous, this association between three such different individuals! One had only to cease to be useful to the other two and it would all break down. But the days went by with this comprise arrangement, a convenience for my continued survival. Eudes was always first to return from his escapades, which he bitterly rued. He would then confess to me his regret that he had not been ruled, like me, by wisdom. With the aid of a little notebook that he passed to me for every question and answer, we used to have long nocturnal conversations – sometimes going on till morning – until Fulbert came home. Then, the sound of my words was like an interminable monologue, despite that constant attentiveness, that other silent voice that never ceased to endorse or contradict me. Oh, what an endless exchange of contradictory ideas, of confused impressions, amid clouds of tobacco-smoke! All it ever led to was to convince me of the impossibility of establishing any real point of contact between us. Were we not like the two banks of a river? From time to time, a bridge would span it, and strangers pass over it, but neither he nor I could ever cross it. If one of the banks had been able to touch the other there would have been no more bridges, no more river.

Eudes believed he could resolve the problem of his life by resolving the problems of his art.

'The only truth,' he declared, 'lies in appearances.'

And I, for whom the world had been transformed

because I had changed my eyes, was inclined to believe him. But my hand on the table belied this assertion.

'As you well know, my dear Eudes,' I retorted with a certain weariness, 'I have only to squeeze this ash-tray between my fingers to refute those words ... What are appearances if a simple gesture can destroy them?'

My friend shrugged his shoulders. 'You're a monster,' he wrote in the notebook, laughing. 'Monsters don't prove anything . . .'

'On the contrary,' I felt like replying, 'they are the only proof!'

I knew that evidently the exception invalidates the rule. I knew that the real world was not the one on which Eudes rested his gaze, perhaps not even the one my own eyes revealed to me. Without being able to imagine it, I conceived of an indestructible world. This world must exist, since I had a presentiment, a prevision of it every day, without any effort. But I was too fond of Eudes, and I dared not bring myself to rob him of his illusion. Had it not for a long time been mine? My dear companion, of such amen-ability, despite your incurable laziness, your artless vanity! Sometimes, in the course of our work, it seemed to me we were within a hair's breadth of that imperishable universe whose reflection was familiar to me, that we were about to touch it. His hand so diligently obeyed my instructions I thought I was at last about to behold the pure masterpiece, conceived by me and realized by him, that would have saved us both. But alas! As soon as he had turned his back, I, in frustration, hastened to destroy this paltry effort and its dangerous fraudulence.

Eudes and I still had one thing in common: despite its anomalies, he liked our mode of life. Fulbert, on the other hand, only came and stood behind his counter because he was obliged to. Without knowing whether to be sorry or glad about it, we ended up with the feeling that one day he would leave us. Fulbert understood nothing of the complexities of us restless aesthetes. To fulfil his capabilities, he needed to be head of a family, to submit himself to a role, and all this to be engraved in marble, not traced in water at the mercy of the slightest breeze. He could only feel comfortable in a world built with his owns hands, with solid foundations. If he let himself get involved in amorous affairs, it was solely because, for him, women represented the means of his redemption, that which bound him to the earth.

Thinking only of the calm that would follow his departure, I had not anticipated the real amputation it was going to be. For Fulbert left us, and sooner than we had imagined. It was like having one part of myself go off, to leave me better confronted with that other part of myself: Eudes. What cries of relief on the first day! We spent the evening mocking the conventionalism that been our friend's downfall.

'He's got just what he deserves!' Eudes chanted. (Yet I knew he envied Fulbert for having dared what he would never have the courage to do. Were they not both tired of this sick-nursing life that I forced on them?)

But the next day we, who were in the habit of

sleeping in, while Fulbert got up early, and took care in opening the shop and keeping it clean and tidy, began to realize what his disappearance was going to mean for us.

'No more art for art's sake, no more taking it easy, my dear Eudes, you're going to have to knuckle down to it now!' I said with feigned irony.

There could be no question of my taking Fulbert's place since all his work was manual. The entire burden of his absence fell on poor Eudes. But I wondered how far the patience of my friend Eudes, who was weaker and more irascible than Fulbert, would extend. Knowing him to be cowardly enough never to admit the true reasons for what he did, perverse and cunning enough to hide his resentment beneath a show of friendship right up to the last day, I was already wondering in what manner he, too, would desert me.

After a little while I became aware of his total incompetence aside from moulding figurines. They were his excuse for making no attempt to do anything useful. Since my only real need was that he should stay with me, I chose to humour his proclivities rather than urge on him tasks that were not to his liking. Yet some exertion might have made him less self-centred. But did I really want him any other way? I approved of his being different from Fulbert, although his irresponsibility frightened me a little, whereas our departed friend, by contrast, with his aptitude for resolving practical problems, was always reassuring. Since we had enough money to live on for several years without worry, I hypocritically told

131

Eudes how much it pained me to see him wasting his talents doing tedious little jobs and he immediately agreed to close the shop. Were not the customers more of a nuisance than a source of any real benefit? We opened up the two rooms by knocking down the partition wall, which got rid of my henceforth unnecessary grille. What a big studio we now had! How delightful to spend all day long idling over a few sketches.

Not having to bother any more about pleasing customers, he gave free rein to his artistic inclinations, devoting himself solely to nudes, preferably female. This obsession led him to an easy licentiousness, verging on pornography, and rather than correct his taste, I pretended to go into raptures over his productions. In any case, he made it plain he was sole master of his work. Faced with his greater satisfaction when guided by his own inspiration, I had given up all form of collaboration. So, knowingly and contemptibly, I encouraged his vices, hoping to make more enjoyable the time he spent with me.

I surely succeeded for his excursions became less frequent. He took real pleasure in his work, and soon the studio was crowded with a multitude of Venuses proffering their rumps or flaunting their breasts. For me, all these immature and monstrous-looking figures assumed a greenish halo sometimes tinged with pink. It was as if I were living in a greenhouse, among a collection of exotic plants of strange forms and unexpected flowerings. They must have made a different impression on Eudes. He would get up every morning very excited at being surrounded by

132

the figurines engendered by his sick mind. But the range of poses suggested to him by his imagination was quickly exhausted. One evening as his pencil remained suspended over a sheet of paper covered with shapeless squiggles, speaking in an undertone that I was intended to hear, he expressed the desire for a model, a real live model. Having given in to all of his whims till then, I could not refuse him this one. Any denial, I knew, would have meant condemning myself to solitude.

As Eudes went off down the street the next day, I wondered from which display window of the outside world he would steal the living mannequin that was to give him fresh inspiration, from which café terrace he would bring home some poor creature in search of a place to live. Under the cloak of Art, his deeds were dictated only by the basest of instincts. I was appalled by this degeneration of a mind whose nobility had won my admiration, as though by the vision of a universe forsaken by its creator and rushing headlong towards its own destruction. The beginning of this decline coincided with Fulbert's departure. That simple-minded young man had been the indispensable ballast on our wandering balloon, the pilot of our unseeing basket, guiding it with a sure hand. When he was no longer there, Eudes became more demanding day by day until my space in the studio was reduced to this meagre stool upon which I reflected on thoughts of our downfall with a look in my eye of apathy and glumness. It was certainly a grave mistake not to made a stand against the seeds of corruption right from the start. They had spread like viburnum with its countless invasive tendrils, covering the refuge where we lived with an inextricable entanglement.

The sound of a key in the lock announcing Eudes' return roused me from my thoughts. I was at once greatly intrigued by the strange attendance accompanying him. It sounded like the raucous blast of a furnace. Hardly had the door opened when a huge Great Dane, spotted like a leopard, came bursting into the middle of the room. There it sat on its haunches, its gaze turned in my direction, and slowly the infernal sound coming from its open mouth – from which hung a tongue of awesome size – quietened down. No doubt it had just exerted itself by running a long way. Yet Eudes, who held this unlikely animal on a leash, did not appear to have been running. Indeed, his composure was striking beside the mastiff's excitement: what inconceivable events did this portend?

Nevertheless, I did not question him, so as not to reveal my impatience. Whatever he might bring into the studio from now on could not but be a cause of conflict between us. I was only there by virtue of his kind-heartedness. Eudes was entitled to my compliance. I knew how consuming a passion his vocation was, and had I not shown every indulgence to the whims it inspired in him? But Eudes took no notice at all of my eloquent silence, although his eyes continued to stare at me. And all of a sudden I realized I was not the object of their attention. What they were staring at lay beyond me. And as I registered this, I simultaneously became aware of another gaze meeting his, the gaze of a stranger, behind me. There I was, between those two gazes, like a transparent target through which they confronted each other.

Then abruptly turning round, I saw, in a face the colour of copper, two black eyes, of the night's impenetrable blackness after the fireworks are over. They were the eyes of a woman crouched on the ground, with her legs tightly clasped by her naked arms. In the gloom, her knees gleamed like apples below her face. How had this woman got in? Had she come through the door unseen, when the dog bounded into the room? I did not attempt to fathom this mystery. Her long, dark hair concealing her clothes made her look like some fabulous animal with bleeding lips. I must have looked quite ridiculous, perched on my stool between those two splendid beasts – the woman and the dog – beneath the silent gaze of my last remaining friend.

This was the beginning of a most improbable life. Loulou and Governor – the names of the girl and the Great Dane – did not merely add a romantic element to the scene of our thoughts and actions. These living entities had their own individuality with which we had constantly to come to terms. I knew, and I think Eudes knew just as well, that they were both there to destroy us. Relations between us began as a secret battle in which no one would admit his plans (but in this obscure conflict was I not myself the fiercest enemy?)

Accommodating these two new tenants was no small matter. Eudes and I had previously knocked down the dividing wall to increase the size of studio when the shop became obsolete, and now what we should have been doing was erecting several dividing walls to partition off our lives. My stool was consigned to a corner to make way for the huge divan on which Loulou was to hold sway. The counter, on which I slept, was pushed back, beside my stool. Governor took up abode inside this very counter, which made a comfortable kennel for him. As for Eudes' armchair, it was relegated, along with his table, modelling stand, and tools, to the far side of the divan, which thus served to separate our now respective domains.

Evidently, the studio was big enough to contain us all, but the unruliness peculiar to each of us – and we were no ordinary beings – made me apprehensive from the outset of the impingements and intimacies that being thrown together like this would entail. The day after her arrival, while she was putting on a pair of stockings taken from her handbag, Loulou took me to task because, she said, I was watching her too closely. At the sound of her voice, Governor, springing out from the counter, began to leap over the divan, knocking several figurines off the shelves, which smashed on the ground. Wanting to intervene, I so forgot myself that I grabbed the ashtray in front of me. It immediately turned to dust. At the sight of this, Loulou began to let out genuine screams, and to jig up and down like a madwoman, standing on the divan.

The effect of this spectacle was to enrage my phlegmatic friend: seizing a lump of clay, he threw it in the girl's direction. Very luckily missing its target, this projectile struck a plaster Leda that in turn fell over and broke with a dull sound. That was as far as this first incident went. That evening, by common accord, we rigged up a system of curtains to divide our room into three separate spaces, hiding the divan and its occupant from my view and Eudes', thus catering to her dangerous modesty.

We were unable to put this system to the test for the very good reason that, the moment she woke up, the first thing Loulou did was to draw back the curtains separating her from us. Within the moving folds of her cubicle, she must have been assailed by the worst terrors. At the sound of the curtains being drawn, Governor would leap over the divan and the pandemonium would start again. There were diabolical scenes whose beauty, visible only to me, left me panting for the rest of the day. Loulou, with her dishevelled and whirling hair, electric shocks running through her pliant body, and the Great Dane's sinewy, heavy mass literally flying round, and all the fragile objects shattering in a din of mingled screaming and barking – all this was like some extraordinary vision born of a poet's frenzied imagination. Having learned to control myself, I remained a mere spectator to this commotion. My hands were once more well behaved and I am sure that Loulou now set off this riotousness only in the attempt to push me over the brink, to check whether she had not been the victim of an illusion that first day, when she saw the ashtray disintegrate between my fingers. But she got nothing for her pains. And although occasionally I still gave her the impression of being a strange character, the rest of the time I almost seemed to her to be just like any other man. Seeing Eudes as an artist, she was more fascinated by him.

One morning, on awakening, I heard the curtain separating Eudes from the divan slowly open, while mine remained closed. What was going on there, behind it, in my absence? With my senses keyed, unable to help myself from making the wildest assumptions, I crept to the end of my bed and with bated breath ventured to peek through to the other side.

What on earth were Eudes and Loulou up to! I would never have believed such childishness could have so enthralled them. And they seemed so utterly spellbound by their game! As far as I could see, this is what it consisted of: the two of them were kneeling on either side of the divan (all I could see of my friend was his thin back, whereas Loulou had her brown face turned towards me, with rapturous eyes lost in that black mop of hair), and they each had in their hands a figurine that appeared to be the focus of their activity. While Loulou fondled hers, cradled it against her breast, covering it with kisses, like a little girl playing with her doll, Eudes, armed with a sharp-pointed puncher, riddled his with holes. After a few minutes they would exchange their statuettes and the game would start again, but this time it was Eudes who ludicrously aped the effusions of maternal love, while Loulou, with the puncher, attacked the statuette now in her hands. In this way, this same figurine was subjected to torture, alternately, by each of them. It was already disintegrating under the puncher, whereas the other retained its original form intact. And throughout this bizarre game, whose significance I failed to comprehend, the two partners' breasts heaved as if with exertion, and there was an expression of delirium on their faces. Watching their frantic gestures, I was wondering what pitch this steadily increasing, crazy excitement was going to reach, when suddenly Loulou stood up and with an air of the utmost indifference went and placed the intact figurine on the bedside table, while Eudes threw to the ground the remains of the other and kicked them away.

This abrupt change in their behaviour had a surprising effect on me: violently tearing back the curtain, I grabbed the statuette that had been put on the table by the divan. I was at once left with nothing between my fingers but a fistful of fine dust. In one fell swoop what I had achieved by my prudence was nullified! What I had been trying not to do in Loulou's presence, I had now just done, of my own free will, like a provocation. Then I looked round. Eudes' eyes were filled with hatred, while gleaming in the woman's eyes was the same dull, charcoal glint, the same dark, velvety fathomlessness as on the day she arrived. Their two faces straining towards me were scaring, as if I had just committed the worst of crimes. I hastily returned to my corner and curtained myself off, hoping the witnesses to my absurd deed would forget about it or think my appearance due to a disturbance of their senses. Perhaps it was.

Silence invaded the studio, but a silence so heavy

that my heart counted the seconds. Knowing of the curse that afflicted me, this young woman would not stay on here another hour, and Eudes would go after her. I now knew what Fulbert and Eudes had wanted to do for me when I met them on the road: to give me the illusion that I could have a life, *nevertheless*. This illusion, my own hands, my destructive, annihilating hands, had just destroyed. I was seated on my stool, with sagging arms and eyes closed, overwhelmed by these thoughts, when the very soft weight of some living thing on my knee made me open my eyes. Before me stood Governor, with his muzzle two inches from my face and his paw on my lap, his heavy paw that had settled there like a bird. With infinite care I ran my hand over his fur. The animal contentment in his gaze revealed to me a friend, my only friend.

I remembered how he had come and planted himself in front of me when he came bursting into the studio. I should have known then, from that moment. This brute beast's strength was uncontaminated, alien to the atmosphere that had been poisoning the studio since Fulbert's departure. Governor had come up to me that first day so that I should see beneath his apparent fierceness the bond uniting us – that toughness, that rigour – which I now clearly recognized. Faced with the remarkable straightforwardness of those enormous jaws and those ridiculously small eyes, faced with the look of that poor big mutt imprisoned in its own strength, I saw again the crudely fitted-together planks of the closed door to the attic where Dr Fohat had received me, I saw again the devastating expression in the old floor-cleaner's eyes, and Edith's face. This rush of memories – memories of elsewhere, memories of before – prompted in me a feeling of loathing for this foul place, this airless closet where I lived in the company of an hysterical tart and a third-rate artist. Using my mouth and, with extreme caution, my fingers, I tied Governor's leash to my belt. Then we set out together, silently.

It was still dark, and I registered this with surprise, for I thought daybreak had long since come. But perhaps this outside darkness was only a projection of the darkness stirring its phantasms inside me? I let myself be guided down the empty street by Governor's proud and supple progress. The town was like a quiet port in which large ships had cast anchor for eternity.

'Governor,' I murmured, 'Governor, take me away from here . . .'

But after wandering round the neighbouring streets, he soon brought me back to our point of departure. We could not escape this quagmire, this slough. It was as if nothing had happened. Had this short walk and the events that preceded it happened only in a dream? Loulou was still there. I found her naked but for her abundant mane of hair, standing motionless on the divan, while Eudes laboured away, with sweat on his brow. Poor boy! Since finding his model he had been struggling to no avail, on paper or with clay, for the sight of this woman incapacitated him. These sessions when she posed for him usually

141

ended in private orgies that Governor accompanied with barking, and to which I strove to remain indifferent. I was more and more sickened by all this.

After that day I resolved to repeat my nocturnal escapade with the Great Dane every so often. The darkness outside refreshed my spirits. On several occasions we encountered tardy pedestrians who fled or hid in terror as we came by. About this time a legend grew up, around where we lived, of a huge-headed leopard that roamed the neighbourhood every night, trailing a ghost after it. It was also about this time that the accident occurred, all that unwholesomeness that had been gathering round me since Fulbert's departure coming to a head.

On my excursions with Governor, I tried not to let my thoughts dwell on the scenes in the studio. In what vices, what acts of depravity were the two accomplices indulging, in my absence? I never knew. One night, as we were approaching the door, Governor suddenly came to a halt and began to howl appallingly. Since he balked at going the few yards separating him from the studio, I freed myself from his leash and, extremely intrigued, entered the silent room alone. Both curtains were open and, stretched out motionless on the divan, amid the untidiness of sheets and blankets spilling onto the floor, lay Eudes, his body completely covered with tiny red pricks. His life had seeped out through these perforations. I picked up the deadly puncher at my feet.

Loulou was hiding under the counter, where the dog belonged. Her bulging eyes were filled with denial. Of what? All his life, Eudes had done nothing but slowly kill himself: he had finally succeeded. What connection could there possibly be between his death and this frightened female? Was all this not bound to happen? Had all this not already happened? Was it necessary to add further punishment to a crime that bore its own punishment within it? As soon as Loulou realized that I was not accusing her, she emerged from the dog-kennel, shaking herself down. Emanating from her hair, as from an overturned jug, came the smell of her flesh. My hands knotted themselves together behind my back at the sight of this splendid body accustomed to living with the utmost freedom. She came closer and closer, and I watched her move in a reddish shimmer.

'What do you want of me?' I asked.

When from her lips came the words, 'I know that you think of me day and night', I then murmured to myself, 'Perhaps.'

That she should speak to me in this way actually came as so little of a surprise that a feverish disquiet came over me, as when confronted with a long-anticipated obstacle, which finds you as ill-prepared as you were at the start. I had forgotten about the corpse concealed behind the curtain. I had forgotten about Governor running around outside. I had forgotten – long forgotten – about Dr Fohat and the law governing my life.

'Only you know how beautiful I am,' she went on, 'and it's only for your sake that I stayed in this dump for so long . . . You knew, oh, yes, you knew! But your pitiful companion had to die before I had the right at last to tell you so. Both you and Governor, that wretched cur that stays with me like a nasty thought, sure enough despised us! You sure enough hated us, on your strolls beneath the untainted stars, eh? And yet it was me and Eudes you were thinking of at every second, and it was back to me the nice, fierce, faithful doggy brought you after your little sentimental wanderings.'

Yes, all this was true, seemed true. I thrashed about in the snare of these words. In my innermost being an angel cried out as it fled. I listened to its cries of protest and despair die away. Soon I would be left again in ultimate solitude, to face this demon of flesh. And I would have to speak in the silence, try to recall those cries already muffled by the silence. How was I to explain to this girl that although she was not wrong, neither was she altogether right? How was I to demonstrate to her that her truth was not exactly the same as mine? She put a finger to her lips and drawing an embroidered case from the warmest and most secret part of her belt, she opened it mysteriously. It contained a pair of spectacles.

No sooner were those lenses in front of my eyes than I felt as if I had become short-sighted again. The halo encircling things, the transparent flames leaping from Loulou's very close face and framing her body, all this shimmering, this light I had eventually got used to — none of it existed any more. As before, I was surrounded by shadow. My eyes lost their special virtue, and I recognized in Loulou, half-naked before me, one of those sordid creatures that used to infest the area around the square. But something about her touched me, filled me with both pity and desire. There was nothing demonic about her eyes any more that were lit only with a covetousness that was entirely human.

'Such weakness! Such submission to its own laws in this fleeting flesh!' I said to myself with emotion. The smell of her hair was the smell of the grave, and all the beauty still poised there, all this fragile beauty would be lost, lost for ever! But it encircled me in a manifold embrace, it enveloped me. Beyond all conscience, I succumbed to its appeal. My hands seized her face, attached themselves to this splendour. For a second I felt her body tremble, then I had the impression that my arms could no longer contain it, that it was expanding in an instantaneous explosion of cosmic proportions. The law I had forgotten was inexorable.

I stared, horrified, at my clothes, now powdered with a fine dust. Loulou, my every moment's desire, thought, obsession, had ceased to exist. Nothing remained of that apparition, nothing but the grotesque spectacles placed over my eyes, which I dared not remove for fear of destroying them as well. I was alone within these forbidding walls. I had lived in this place for days and nights, for entire months. Furiously I grabbed hold of everything around me, and soon there was nothing left in the studio but this fine and quickly vanishing dust that was all too familiar to me. A single moment's hesitation kept my heavy hands – these tools of destruction – suspended over my friend's corpse. He looked horrible, as though eaten by an army of red ants. But I had lost all respect for death and for myself. I wanted to carry my rebellion to the extreme. For a moment a spark of hope flashed through me. What if this body which was no longer of this world were to give me what life denied me: the right to take, the right to seize? Alas! I had no sooner framed the thought than I was left with nothing but a cloud of dust in my arms. Oh, the surge of manic laughter that overcame me after that, the horrifying glee that made me dance round the deserted studio to the point of exhaustion! Everything that had been my life, my hope of life, our ardent discussions, our fierce hatred and our love were now no more than impalpable dust. Amid this destitution I suddenly remembered Governor, and I crawled over to the door, where I called out in a voice drained of strength. But like the studio, like my heart and brain, the street was empty.

From this emptiness the invisible forces of evil soon brought forth abject thoughts. With the arrival of daybreak they sprouted into venomous clumps. All I needed to do to regain my reason for living was to take off the glasses. But this was something I did not want to do any more. What did I care for the wonderful world I had glimpsed, since nothing would save me from the nefarious power that was the price I had to pay for it? Better to make free use of this power – the one thing that remained to me! A chill dawn cast light, in the deserted studio, on objects that had reverted to their former appearance. While overwhelming me with unlimited despair, this humdrum reality, this emptiness, this vacancy also cheered me with a sneaking exuberance. Alone! I was

now sole master of my actions. With no witness to
judge their consequences! It occurred to me to use, to
please myself, the curse I had been languishing under
as though it were some misfortune. With unsalutary
haste I laid hands on the shutters and locks, on
everything that prevented the daylight and life
outside from entering the place. A broad laugh, a
murderer's laugh, distorted my mouth. I discovered
that my power could after all serve my personal satisfaction. And like a wolf biding its time in the fold,
seated on a counter, keeping open the shop, a
tradesman without any goods, I awaited the return
of the customers.

Pretty perfumed customers! Eternal shoppers!
They all came back – those who had turned Fulbert's
head, those who had killed Eudes.

'No, ladies, the gentleman who used to run the
shop isn't here any more, nor is the artist. I'm sole
master now!'

Oh, their admiring glances, their lovely dewy-eyed
looks of tenderness and lust!

'We've no more figurines for sale, ladies, pretty
ladies! There are no tools left for sculpting them, no
clay for modelling them, no hands to make them . . .
But we'll have some tomorrow, ladies, or the next
day . . . You can trust my word . . . As sure as you're
pretty, I swear to you . . . pretty you are . . .'

A familiar refrain, the same old song my two companions had sung, one after the other, in my presence. Oh, I knew it well! They all fell for it. They
always would!

'For you, my dear Lydia, I have one pretty little

figurine left . . . just one . . . a sweet little cherub, a darling little porcelain cherub that I kept aside . . . just for you . . . It's a bit delicate, but I know you'll take care of it . . . Come back this evening when I'm alone . . . You can have it as a present . . . Come back this evening!'

And sure enough, Lydia came back. And so did Yolande, and Mathilde, and Julienne. They all came back, one after the other, to fetch the one, last, delicate, precious little figurine. And for a fleeting moment, the time it took for a swift kiss, I hugged them to my breast, every one of them. On my breast they exploded into spirals, into beams, into cloud, a wonderful cloud of light smoke. Like Loulou. Nothing survived, not even the memory of their dresses, their blouses, their lacy frills . . . For, every time, after every session, I would weep, weep until morning, into these silky repositories of their fragrance. And when morning came all that was left in my clenched fingers was a grey shadow, a shadow dispelled by the draught from the street when I opened the door again.

'Hurry, pretty customers! I'm keeping aside for each of you the prettiest figurine, the one and only, the rarest of the rare! For each of you!'

There was Giselle, and Annie, and Elise. And there was an endless embrace carried on every evening, and every evening interrupted, a monstrous wrestling bout, a tussle between two living beings, a man and a woman, that left, in the ever empty studio, only an ever-greater accumulation of ghosts. Figures that no sooner appeared than vanished, dream images taken back into the dream – oh, would that you had been just the fleeting materializations of my imagination! Evening would send me out into the dark streets, with yet darker schemes in mind, a helpless shadow in pursuit of shadows. A rustling of fabric set me off like a bloodhound, scenting my victim by the way she walked, assessing her defensiveness or passivity. I was drawn into the most shameful arrangements, the sad hero of adventures not to be spoken of ... I lived surrounded by remnants swallowed up by the dark. I made love with the dark. A dark-handed shadow leading the dance of the shadows. Shadows stolen from the darkness and returning to darkness. But it was never dark enough or gloomy enough to hide their faces while wrestling with the shadow.

One day when I was wondering whether I would have the patience to wait till evening, so reckless had I grown in my desires, a huge animal came bursting into the shop and leapt at my face. This attack sent my glasses flying. With the recovery of my former vision, I was at once completely bedazzled. The woman before me now breathed in the midst of a veritable shimmering of pinks and milky white, and my feelings towards her were totally transformed. My response to the glory of her quivering flesh was unguarded admiration. I was overwhelmed with such a sense of purity that tears flowed from my eyes at the thought of my cynicism and infamy. My sweetheart must have understood the change wrought on my intentions.

'Goodbye!' was the only word she uttered as she turned on her heel.

Was there not some regret, some disappointment in her going? And yet her life was being restored to her! After she had left the shop, I recognized Governor at my feet. He was foaming as if having run a long way. His panting surrounded his body with a steel-coloured nimbus streaked with black and somehow sparklingly iridescent. For a moment I felt a desire to try out my power on this beast, to annihilate this mass of muscle as well. But before that trusting gaze innocent of any effrontery, I immediately dismissed this wicked thought. The exuberant demonstration of affection the Great Dane had just offered me in breaking my glasses was the sign of a new course. Oh, the sudden hope that I might be forgiven for everything! This quiescent force, ready to leap up again, instilled me with profound contentment of the kind obtained by a firm resolve. For a long time I skimmed his coat with my hand, surprised myself that I resisted temptation. But his eyes remained so full of trust and love! I succumbed to their expression. I melted at the sweetness of this contentment.

'Good dog,' I murmured, 'you're my dog, I only want to obey you. Wherever your journey may now lead me, I shall follow you, Governor!'

It was neither morning nor evening, but night as bright as noontide in an unreal land of ice, a night like our nights of old. This time there would be no coming back.

'The time has come, Governor, your time has come!'

After attaching the leash to my belt, I tightly locked my murderous hands together behind my back. The Great Dane had immediately risen and when it felt me harnessed to its powerful neck, it bounded forward. I let myself be carried along by its agile legs, by the majestic movement, that might have been winged, of its sinewy body. It seemed as though the great night of the outside world mysteriously opened its portals to let us pass. The moon made every facet of this black-diamond world sparkle. Until morning I allowed myself to be led towards a destination unknown to me, but that I knew to be mine. Now and again, the leash between us relaxed its tension, either because I, borne on by the momentum, continued to advance, or Governor, hesitating, suddenly stopped to sniff at the paving stones, to put his nose to the wind. Then, like a blind man, I would feel lost for ever in permanent darkness. But the jerk of the leash, taut once more, or the barking ahead of me – however distant it sometimes seemed – reminded me that someone else was responsible for guiding me. Perhaps to a new life where it would be possible for me to live again, in a different guise, purged of remorse for this life.

The first rays of dawn found Governor sitting in front of a gateway. It was ajar, and we entered its gloominess. I recognized with no surprise the dank courtyard and staircase. It was the third time I set eyes on these premises! Since the Great Dane was circling round and I could not free myself from his leash, I shouted, 'Stop, Governor, stop!'

His barking drowned out my voice and I was

quaking at the idea that it was going to waken the whole neighbourhood. It reverberated between the walls on which dawn cast a pale light, reflected back a hundred times as though by echoes in a cave.

'Quiet, Governor, quiet!'

My admonishments made him howl all the more. Suddenly a door opened and the old woman in the jacket, who must have been the caretaker, appeared. I saw rather than heard her shout abuse at me. What I am certain of is that she pulled the most horrible faces. Yet in all this hullabaloo I thought I discerned the name of Dr Fohat, and I had no doubt that what the old woman had to tell me was of the utmost importance, but how was I to hear it? At last I managed to free myself and with one bound I leapt on to the staircase. I just had time to see the old woman sneer and make a gesture at me, before shutting her door again, leaving to Governor the rumpus-filled courtyard.

I climbed one storey, two storeys, and stopped to catch my breath, leaning against some kind of large oriental vase that happened to be there. Then suddenly I jumped: the vase had just moved beneath me, and I caught a glimpse in the semi-darkness of the huge head of a cayman whose languid, little blue eyes were staring at me. I raced upstairs as if I had the devil on my tail. There, on the landing, which I reached without having recovered my breath, was a slimy mass in the form of a bear but covered with scales. This hideous beast was moving slowly. Terrified, I went hurtling downstairs again. I had to climb over the cayman that was now completely blocking the way. And as I went down and down, making use of the banister, even this banister seemed to start moving. Then I snatched away my hand, scared out my wits: what I had taken for a banister were enormous snakes strung out like creepers from one stairpost to the other. The head of the one I had just touched reared up, yawning, two inches from my face. I took in a single leap the last five steps between me and the ground floor. A whole seething mass of foul beasts continued to appear, issuing from every recess, every nook and cranny, as I dashed through the courtyard. I caught a momentary glimpse of the caretaker, at her door, with her hands on her hips, laughing rudely. My panic did not allow me to fasten the leash to my belt again, and I jumped astride Governor's haunches, who doubtless was waiting for this, to get out of this menagerie fast.

The livid dawn I had seen breaking must have been just an apparition of the moon between two clouds, or perhaps I had remained a whole day in that staircase where terror had robbed me of all notion of time? The fact is that as soon we were outside again, night enveloped us once more. And we forged ahead into the darkness as if there were never to be any further respite for us, covering ground at such a pace, it seemed to me, that in the time it took to draw breath we left behind long streets, jumped over houses, took entire neighbourhoods in one stride, flew over outlying districts. A crazy journey that had already taken us far beyond the town limits. The towers and belfries we were again passing were now those of twenty smaller towns, twenty villages, then another huge town, like the one we had left scarcely a moment ago. Borne on the back of my fabulous mount, I travelled on, from place to place, to the sway of his leaping bounds that weariness did not slacken. And it was indeed Governor that carried me so, that I felt beneath me; they were his flanks streaming between my thighs, and his stiff, pricked-up ears that I gently tickled in the hollow left by the wind.

'Governor, my good dog, will we not arrive soon? Do we have much further to go?'

This murmur from my lips, if he heard it, seemed to hasten rather than slow his pace, and we raced on without stopping, like an arrow, over the sleeping fields. Soon, a fine, stabbing rain began to fall that left me soaked to the bone. But through the millions of drops that turned my clothes to tatters, our journey continued in prodigious strides at an even rhythm. The rain became so heavy that before long I could see nothing around us. Gusts of wind, armed with glass spears, assailed us. We repelled them with the ease of a bird flying through cloud. The wind and rain beat furiously on my bare back and knees, but I cleaved so closely to my mount that the play of my own joints and ligaments were at one with the supple movement of his muscles. At last, as lightning lit up the skies, I saw a broad river before us. Instead of lying slack between its banks, its muddy waters had risen and were running high, like a moving wall. We plunged head first into this liquid universe.

It became instantly calm. Breaking Governor's

momentum, the obstacle reduced our headlong gallop to walking speed – such at least was my immediate impression, for after a few minutes I noticed that in fact my valiant steed was now swimming strenuously. There was no doubt about it, we were fording a wide river. The water, flowing crosswise to the way we were heading, was as heavy above and below as it was on either side of my arms. The tumult of the elements that had surrounded us shortly before was succeeded by the menacing silence of the watery deep. I took advantage of this lull to relieve Governor of my weight and to let myself once again be led by him with the help of the leash.

Curiously, I advanced in an upright posture with no greater difficulty than I would have had walking on dry land, although my body was suspended under water, whereas the Great Dane's progress continued to be accomplished laboriously, at the cost of arduous and constant effort. Occasionally, tree-trunks went by, revealing the speed of the current. One of these swiftly-moving shadows, striking the taut line between Governor and myself, suddenly reared up. And during the few seconds it remained erect, I realized it had a human form, and was not made of rotten wood as I had imagined. Almost at once another struck me full in the chest, and I shuddered at the feeling of hair wrapping itself round my arms like frozen snakes, while a white face skimmed past mine. The eyes in this face were open and I thought I recognized them, but already it had been swept on by the current. The further we advanced, the more numerous these encounters became. When this human flotsam got caught on the line, or bumped into me, I had time to glimpse their faces. And soon I recognized, as they passed in succession, several of the women who used to haunt the studio, and whom I had seduced with deceitful promises. There was Annie again, and Mathilde, and Lydia. And this one here, swirling round in a great eddy of green algae, was Loulou, Loulou with colourless lips and a wan gaze. They came back, in these ghastly forms, from I know not what abyss, were returning to I know not what abyss, perhaps to recover there the rest of the physical appearance they had had on earth.

Soon these faces seemed to emerge from my most distant memories. One, whose body struck me so hard that I was left reeling, was beyond any possible mistake that of a little girl I had held in my arms one day when I ventured into the environs of the square. Was she, too, dead, and must I consider myself responsible for her death, as for all the others? For this procession of drowned women whose bodies caught me in passing looked for all the world like the grotesque parade of my remorse. And yet, although these apparitions around me filled me with an ill-defined sense of despair and bitter repentance, I had no time to dwell on my tardy and futile pangs of conscience. And when a yet more violent shock eventually broke the line connecting me to Governor, I recognized Edith's battered body, rearing up before my eyes like the shadow of some enormous bird.

The current swept away this final vision, like all the others. When I found myself once more where there were fewer drifting dead bodies, I became aware that the Great Dane had disappeared. Swimming on a horizontal plane, he afforded less purchase to all those drowned bodies hindering my progress and, freed of his leash, he had doubtless considerably outdistanced me? How would I manage to rejoin him now? How would I find my way, and what could my way be in this element through which it was my privilege to move with as much ease as before, on land? The glaucous light that had so far allowed me to see was growing dimmer and dimmer. I was, as it were, borne along by this murky turbidness shot through with flashes of light, and at the same time menaced on all sides by the one hundred octopus tentacles of my indecision. Would my sole efforts ever succeed in getting me out of these depths?

In the total darkness in which I advanced, a live darkness that skimmed my body like the lick of night, a distant barking suddenly indicated to me the direction Governor had taken. I headed that way and came up against a wall. With much groping, and endless minutes later, I found some rusted rungs riveted into the wall, and I clung to them as though to a liferaft. At that moment Governor's bark could be heard again, coming from above me, at an even greater distance. Then I began the arduous climb. My hands and feet slipped on the rudimentary ladder, and the current kept threatening to wrench me from the slimy rungs, to cast me back into the dark depths.

After enormous effort I saw a gleam of light a few feet above my head, like that from a basement window. It came through a hole in the wall I had just climbed. Dragging myself up to it, I used the last of my strength to get through this hatch. An eddy of fetid water caught me and I thought I was going to lose my grip, but in that very instant the clear sky dazzled me. The outlet from that cesspool was a gully-hole that I climbed through with delight. What safety! What joy to feel on firm ground now and to see blue skies, simply by raising my head the tiniest bit! Nearby flowed a river that looked like the one in the town where I used to live. I was astonished to find it so narrow, when it had taken me so long to traverse its depths. Barges were moored alongside quays congested with crates and barrels. The total dereliction of the place reassured me and I stretched out for a moment on the paving-stones to warm myself in the sun, happy to breathe the world's air again, to find myself among the stillness of things in their eternal matrix of light.

THE LANTERN

Air is full of transparent images, which are the earth's soul. Light, the source of all life, prevents those images, that only sleep lets us glimpse, from taking shape. Air, the vehicle of sound, can symbolize mobility, lightness, inconstancy. When this fluid called Ether or Heavenly Abyss is left to its own devices, it turns into Nahash, or the serpent in Genesis. It can happen that a person, in breathing, might swallow a fly, and be suffocated by too much air.

I must have slept for a long time. My first thought on waking was of Dr Fohat. If I had escaped without injury so many vicissitudes, it was because of my determination to see him again. He could not be unaware of the cost of his experiment. Perhaps, having discovered the antidote, he would restore my right to a life, without taking from me the marvellous vision I owed to his knowledge? My anxiety for Governor got me back on my feet. I now knew that the Great Dane was the doctor's envoy and was taking me to him.

Behind the congestion on the quays, I could see a huge square, with open shop-windows and café terraces along the far edge of it. How could I avoid attracting attention on this esplanade? As I came closer, I saw that all eyes were upon me. And suddenly the crowd, a few minutes ago a miniature swarm, drew nearer, grew bigger, with raised arms, their faces threatening or laughing. Then I remembered I was naked. With all the agility my legs were capable of, I ran back to hide among the piles of stuff on the riverside. After wandering for a long while between derelict trucks, under the menacing jibs of mechanical hoists, I eventually found some work clothes left behind in a yard by some stevedore, and put them on. Nothing would prevent me now from passing unnoticed. Yet I made a great detour so as not to have to cross the whole width of that empty space again. I need not have bothered: all those people had forgotten my grotesque appearance of just a short while ago, and it was in total freedom that I mingled with them in their animation.

The westering sun gilded the facades, setting the windows ablaze; the dank smell of the river blended with the smells from the stalls; and a weekend gaiety was painted on everyone's face. Crossing several streets packed with this rabble in holiday mood, I came to an almost deserted boulevard. On a bench sat a tramp who, in his tattered clothes, looked so like me he could have been my brother. He offered me a piece of bread that he had been eating. I explained I would gladly accept it, but that a congenital disability prevented me from using my hands. Was I not truly disabled, and more destitute than this poor wretch? Patiently, he fed me each mouthful, as my lost friends, Fulbert and Eudes, had fed me in the past! When I had eaten enough, I gazed for a long time at the phosphorescent lights the night wind kindled in the leaves just for me.

'What a magnificent display!' I murmured. 'Are you not thrilled by this magnificence?'

The look the tramp gave me was the look he might have given a harmless simpleton, and I got up to my feet to continue my journey.

A little further on my attention was caught by some two dozen people, standing and staring open-mouthed beneath some Argand lamps. On a platform in their midst a magician – or so he claimed to be –

was performing conjuring tricks. But so great was his incompetence, or so profound his contempt for those watching him, that the secret of his childish sleights of hand was at once detectable without need of any particular astuteness. The crude manipulation he displayed, generously larded with patter, would have put to flight a less gullible audience, but these spectators were enjoying the performance in all naivety. I was about to leave when this charlatan called out to me, doubtless because of the togs I had on, taking me to be the humblest of port workers.

'Hey, you! The elegant gentleman over there! Won't you come up on to the platform . . .'

All eyes turned towards me and I realized that the best thing was to comply, so as not to awaken any further interest. So I climbed up next to the fellow.

Now addressing the crowd, he shouted, 'In two shakes of a lamb's tail, I shall make the glass bowl you see on this table disappear.'

So saying, and with much gesturing, he simply covered the bowl with a black cloth. The circle of viewers applauded as if in the face of a miracle.

'But that's not all, ladies and gentlemen, I'm going to make this magic bowl that has now disappeared before your eyes reappear in just a moment in the hands of this elegant gentleman who has been good enough to lend me his kind assistance.'

And as he pronounced these words, he slipped into my hands the glass bowl, still wrapped in the cloth making it invisible. That was rash of him! My fingers had no sooner closed around it than it really did vanish this time, obliterated by my touch. And when the unfortunate fellow lifted the cloth, my hands were empty. Instead of bursting out laughing, the audience seemed disconcerted. To add to their confusion, the conjurer, himself bewildered and thinking he had been made a fool of, accused me of theft. Seeing that things were going badly, I knocked over the lanterns and fairly barging my way through the assembled crowd I fled into the darkness.

My pursuers, with the conjurer in the lead, collected up passers-by, and I soon had a real mob on my tail, shouting, 'Stop, thief!' Along with this cry, I thought I occasionally heard the cry of 'Stop, murderer!' Although my conscience was not entirely clear, I felt as if I had landed on another planet and was being chased by a horde that belonged to a species different from my own. Was not such bitterness and hatred in these cries inexplicable? These men whose stupid faces I could picture before me could not be my fellow human beings. For them, any conjuring trick was permissible, as long as the sleight of hand was clearly visible, the strings apparent, the mystery without mystery. These thoughts and my profound dejection tended to slow me down. I could not convince myself of my guilt, so unreal a quality did the scene on the platform, in its speed and unexpectedness, have. It was not possible that this little misapprehension, this misunderstanding apparently unrelated to my previous crimes, should have set the town after me in this way. The longer I kept running away, the more the idea grew inside me that by running away I was losing the last chance to clear myself. So I was on the point of letting myself be caught, torn to pieces perhaps, when a very familiar bark and Governor's panting, almost right next to me, bucked my spirits.

At his side I picked up speed, and the hue and cry of those chasing me became more distant. When they were no more than a faint, indistinct sound, I let myself drop to the ground, exhausted. We must have been very far from our point of departure and the pitch darkness protected us. Tiredness made me fall into a torpor filled with hallucinations. Was the night already over when Governor's breath roused me from this haunted sleep? I was not a little surprised to see that we were still in the labyrinth of the quayside. So we had only gone round in a circle, like beasts caught in a trap. The diffuse glimmerings of dawn cast a soft-coloured mist just above the ground.

'Faithful Governor! Time to go! Let's not stay a minute longer in this chaos! Let's go, my strong, powerful dog!'

He looked as if he had just had a long rest although he had not slept a wink, I was sure of it. Full of eagerness, he kept jumping over hurdles like a spaniel, returning to lick the ground at my feet.

'Let's go, Governor, quietly now, my fine creature, let's go.'

We set off side by side this time, like good hunters alert to the same prey.

'Dawn hunters, we are, lovers of first light, aren't we, Governor? Sometimes we set out in the evening, sometimes at night, but always before dawn, so as always to find ourselves together before the rising sun, cleansed by the dew, I feeling cheerful and you,

Governor, frisky, and both of us so alone! So as always to salute together the first shot of rosiness in the midst of the darkness, like today, Governor, like today!'

In a single stride, it seemed to me, we left behind the neighbourhoods that I had ventured into the day before. The tramp I had thought to be my brother was still stretched out on his bench, like an empty bag by a dustbin. Further on, torn handbills fluttered round the deserted platform like the feathers of a dead bird. It was here that the crowd almost got the better of me . . .

'With you, Governor, I have no fear. Gallant Governor, you're the one who is my brother.'

These litanies comforted me. Streets gave way to more streets, and we went through an endless suburb, as though invincibly drawn on. But soon, as it grew lighter, more threatening figures appeared. Whistles and calls echoed behind us, responding to each other as we passed. Above us I heard windows open and close violently. No doubt I had been recognized. The Great Dane, my saviour the previous day, was becoming a dangerous marker. No, it was surely not my nakedness or the power of my hands that incited these people to chase me. Something else, in my features, or my bearing, must prompt their curses. A surly mob was gathering again, growing at every turning. The increasingly narrow and congested streets prevented us from going any faster. Their bustle, quickly turning hostile, closed in on us. We were now hurrying along winding lanes with no pavements, the wan light of day barely reaching down to the level of our faces. From these dark gullies we emerged lost and disorientated, and so several times we were almost cornered. But Governor stood his ground, menacingly, and the frightened crowd always left us a way out at the last minute. Yet I was aware of the precariousness of this deliverance, and I was overcome with dismay as the horde of our enemies and their baying increased.

All of a sudden a large space opened out as if the walls were making way for us. Carried on by our momentum, we advanced for a few seconds into this emptiness under a dull light. I thought with terror that we were making ourselves easy prey out in the open like this, but just as quickly as the tall buildings had vanished the yelping behind us fell silent. Then looking back, I saw our pursuers, standing still, arrested as though in front of an invisible wall. And as far as I could tell from a distance, their faces were frozen in common fear. I stopped, not understanding, uneasy despite the joy of having momentarily escaped this mob. Saved? Were we saved? I could not tell what element of luck or misfortune was involved in this unhoped-for deliverance. This was a case of some disturbing miracle. But who would balk at an unknown risk if it saved you from certain and immediate danger? The mysterious constraint preventing our pursuers from reaching us made them crowd together in growing numbers as they emerged from every outlet, as if before a lake that only Governor and I had the privilege of crossing by walking on water. We calmly strolled away from that rabble, already by now a small dark stirring of unrest, back there, way back there, at the foot of the cracked and pale facades that were also disappearing from view, as if the earth, by its movement, were precipitating them into sinking to favour our escape.

And it was then that I discerned less than a hundred metres ahead – was it a mirage? – some kind of huge, greyish palace. Its structure had until then been lost in low cloud. I stopped myself crying out at this apparition that loomed up like a silent steamer emerging out of the fog. Our footsteps made no sound as we walked towards it in the dawn mist. Its countless windows looked like a final, mysterious parade of the stars. Within this extraordinary abode, I was sure of it, Dr Fohat conducted his experiments. To what hypotheses had his research led him? What new revision had his theories undergone? Impatience made me anxious. Nevertheless, the sight of this enormous pile, like some foretaste of the City of the Future, instilled me with the confidence I badly needed after so many reversals. I imagined the strange doctor somewhere in the central part of this building, surrounded by secretaries, typewriters, and telephones, having exchanged his dressing gown for a well-cut jacket . . .

My imagination was running away with me, outpacing my legs. For I had to hurry again, but this time to keep up with Governor, and I ran willingly, as impatient as he was. An image born of the intellect that had taken on the substance of reality, a long concrete facade extended before us now, bizarrely decorated with niches filled with statues. We passed through the tall gate amid graveyard silence. The Great Dane jumped and barked as he had done not so very long ago in the dark, dank courtyard. The certainty of having arrived had him keyed up. But this time his barking was not apprehensive. Yet it rang in my ears like the breathy sound of bugles being practised in barrack yards.

We went under a high archway through a first block of buildings. The massive walls, cast all of a piece, had the appearance of lead or lava. The livid brilliance of the sky coloured the dark surface with greenish pewter reflections. Stretching away beneath this other-worldly light was a great interior courtyard filled with a kind of frozen tumult. For it was as though a crowd, massed in disorder on either side of the central pathway, had just stopped still, at the moment of our arrival. Actually, the crowd consisted of identical statues, all made, from the soles of their boots to the tips of their helmets, of the same material as the entire palace. Led by Governor, I made my way, slightly hesitantly, between these solid mannequins resembling pillars. Their absolutely identical size, their perfect uniformity deprived this theatrical gathering of any human quality.

At the centre, we skirted round a pedestal on which was erected some sort of sugar-loaf mass of the same leaden colour as everything else. And looking back at it, with a distant memory flashing through my mind, I thought this mass could well represent a huge person draped in a coat or long dressing-gown. Retracing my footsteps, I was then able to read this solitary inscription, carved into the pedestal in large letters: ALEXANDRE FOHAT. Sudden illumination! Like a beam of light, this name dissipated the close atmosphere of this strange place.

All at once feeling cheerful, I ran to catch up Governor. And it so happened that just as I came up to the second facade where the Great Dane was already growing impatient, a sudden and this time visible ray, piercing the clouds, made a nickel-plated button on the black rectangle of the entrance sparkle. I pushed it as if I had long been a regular visitor to the place, with all the necessary calmness and firmness – I mean, with the indispensable caution without which my touch would have reduced it to atoms. A catch released the bolt and, pushing open the doors, I found myself in a huge hall (everything here was of superhuman proportions). A light like that in the courtyard prevailed here, although it came through no visible window, and I soon discerned a multitude of names inscribed on the walls. I went up to these lists but I found it absolutely impossible to read a single one of them. Some were composed of a series of identical vowels, others solely of consonants. I was nevertheless able to observe that the characters were not engraved but pasted on to the walls. Some disaster must have caused them to fall to the ground one day, and an ignorant or mischievous hand had put them up again in this illegible disorder.

Putting off till later the task of decoding this puzzle, I headed for the lift, which by itself filled the end of the hall, between two staircases. The lift-cabin took me up, at first slowly, then with increasing speed. Between each floor my eyes looked down through the gate on to the spiral staircase. And suddenly I caught sight of Governor, whom I had completely forgotten. Having caught up with me seemed to excite him, to encourage him to climb even faster, as if he were making it a point of honour not to be left behind. His exertion to climb the countless steps, while I complacently let myself be carried up, reminded me of crossing the river. Here, the injustice was even more flagrant, since I did not even have to move my feet, whereas he had to make an enormous effort to follow me. And in fact he could not manage it, and I saw his despairing eyes one last time as I shot past him. Even his panting, which filled the building, grew distant and faded away, and I continued my ascent amid the gentle hum of that well-oiled piece of engineering.

This monotonous sound eventually made me drowsy, and I think I had completely dozed off when the cabin jolted to a halt, alerting me to the fact that I had arrived. An elderly woman came and opened the lift-gate and I immediately recognized the old servant who, in my presence, had brought Dr Fohat's food to the attic, where our last meeting had taken place. The mere sight of this woman bolstered my confidence and purely as a matter of form I asked whether her master was here. Her sole response was to gaze at me earnestly with a mournful air.

I entered an entirely glass-walled room. Daylight came in on all sides. A tiny table marked the centre of this curious accommodation. I recognized it as the one that had previously furnished the attic and had then seemed huge. Going closer, I saw on it several boxes containing little painted balls of plaster that were probably dolls' eyes. Indeed, next to these boxes, a few heads with empty eye-sockets awaited completion. At that moment an absurd thought came to me: 'Is it possible that I once mistook these miniature eyes for real ones?' No, I refused to believe that Dr Fohat's powers of suggestion could have been so effective. Anyway, I did not dwell on this quaint idea that was beginning to assail me with a certain unease.

A quiet sound overhead led me to assume there must be a terrace above the room. No doubt it was Dr Fohat's tread I had just heard, although its lightness put me more in mind of some winged creature's footstep. I strained my ears and, already a little unnerved by the returned silence and the loneliness of the place, I moved towards the only other door, opposite the entrance. As I reached it, the panels opened of their own accord and I was caught in a strong wind. I had to readjust my breathing to this new atmosphere before taking the risk of stepping out onto the suspended narrow footway. I was not mistaken: rungs linked this aerial catwalk to a terrace. But despite my eagerness to join the inhabitant of this peculiar abode, I was fearful of venturing onto those footrails set between heaven and earth, when a commotion behind me made me look back inside the glass-walled room. Governor was furiously racing round and jumping about the apartment I had just left. It was quite simply the draught caused by his bursting into the room that had opened the door just now.

'Governor!' I cried.

At the sound of my voice, he joined me in a single bound, and before I could stop him, he launched himself on to the aerial rungs, regardless of their being in space. So, without further reflection, I did likewise. We reached the terrace almost simultaneously. What followed took place in a flash. At the far end of the platform we had just climbed on to, I saw a silhouetted figure leaning over the void. Lying at the feet of that figure, looking tiny in that vast expanse, was what appeared to be a bundle of coloured rags. Governor went rushing for that thing, open-jawed, with such fury, an expression of such ferociousness in his little eyes that an irrational fear swept over me. Swifter than him, I lunged forward with my hands outstretched and clung to his neck with all my might to restrain him. At that moment the terrible power of my hands reminded me of its existence. Too late! Governor, my faithful dog, was no more than a memory, a cloud of impalpable dust that the strong wind immediately blew away. And, stunned by the speed and unexpectedness of this turn of events, I must have been staring wild-eyed at the figure before me, when it turned round.

It was a young girl, almost a child. She gazed at me for a moment without showing any surprise, then at the sight of the object lying at her feet, she said, bending down, 'Oh, my doll!'

But, perhaps prompted by the desire to anticipate her gesture, perhaps by the more obscure desire to avenge Governor who had just met his doom because of this trifling bit of cloth, I reached out my arm

faster than she did. Well, this extraordinary phenomenon occurred: the doll remained intact in my
hands. No matter how much I pressed and squeezed
it with great inward excitement, it retained beneath
my fingers its consistency, firmness, solidity, like some
indestructible object.

How could I find words that did not sound like
incoherent stammering? I handed the young girl her
plaything and covered with my tears her free hand,
the little hand she surrendered to me, unknowing.
She was leaning on her elbows over empty space,
with the wind twisting her hair. I could not tire of
feeling her little fingers in mine, of sensing their
firmness and at the same time their extreme soft-
ness, of apprehending their fragility and at the same
time their tremendous resistance: of having control
over this life without destroying it, of registering the
pulsing of this blood without causing it to dry up, of
experiencing this miracle without its immediately
ceasing to exist. I was demented, I wept, I laughed.
And I could hardly wait for the turmoil to fade from
my face so that I could gaze up in happiness at my
liberator. Her hand did not pull away from mine,
and in the end this acquiescence seemed to me as
strange as her silence. Then glancing at her anxiously, I saw her eyes. Oh, what sudden bliss! Boun-
teous grace emanated from them. How had I
remained so long without daring to look at them?
Now I could not tear my gaze away from them. I no
longer saw the smile on that face, its extraordinary
corona and brilliance, I was riveted by her eyes that
dispensed with mere language. She could have

remained for ever silent and I might have lost for ever the very yearning for speech. I, who had been afraid of troubling those eyes by my bewilderment, could see from their unfailing serenity that nothing could dim their luminance. Where did they come from? From what altar of forgiveness had they been stolen to become the adornment of that pure ingenuous face?

I was roused at last from my contemplation by some words of human speech, a voice of a childish timbre. But its inflections were of such disturbing gravity that it immediately reminded me of another voice, a voice that had never ceased to resound in the depths of my memory: that of Dr Fohat. A distant echo of his words – was that all I would find of him in this house?

'I knew you'd come,' said this voice. 'My uncle promised me you would. I've been waiting for you every day, on this terrace. Even today my eyes were scanning the distance, hoping to see you arrive. And all of a sudden . . . now, how did you get here? You were there, behind me . . . I thought you were still so far away, and you were so close!'

This tenuous, grave voice cast these words into space, which seized on them and carried them away. They reached me only in fragments, having circled the globe. This young girl belonged to the realm of air. The sounds that emerged from her mouth radiated in concentric circles like soundwaves transmitting from an aerial. The gusts that blew her black pinafore against her childish body were her companions. Beside this sister of the wind, I must have looked like a disjointed puppet that a suddenly released spring quickly sets free of its strings.

'My name is Lucile,' she said, and these two syllables also belonged to the realm of air.

Already her little hands were drawing me away. We descended the iron ladder with the precision of acrobats, and came running up to the table in the big glass-walled room. At that moment a fleeting memory flashed through my mind. Despite the blur then enveloping them, had I not already seen these magnificent eyes, now illuminating a face, placed before me on this very same whitewood table? At once, like a tilted mirror righting itself, this vision from the past vanished, to blend with the present one that set my heart racing. Lucile! She spoke, and her voice was like a flowering of snowdrops in parched earth. But I did not understand the haste with which she spoke. Her words seemed to have been prepared in advance, like a lesson she had learned and whose message she had to convey to me at all costs. The pitch of her voice, at first just a murmur, gradually rose, although nothing in what she said seemed to necessitate such urgency or importunity. I was unaware how limited our conversation was to be, and did not realize that by speaking louder and louder she was trying to overcome another sound, which was indistinct at first but was to drown these confessions in its tumult before I had time to interrupt them or to investigate their true meaning, by questioning her.

'My uncle, Dr Fohat,' she began, 'adopted me when I was about seven. It was as if I had been incapable of looking at things before knowing him. When I was with him, they appeared in a different light. Being very rich, he did not hesitate to lavish on me the most costly fancies of his imagination or my caprice. This glass-walled room was built on his instructions solely because I needed air and light. I remember that when the desire to be beautiful first came over me – at the age when we young girls usually get this desire – my uncle solemnly promised me magnificent eyes, the most beautiful eyes in the world . . . An old man's foolishness, do you think? And yet I never ceased to believe in his promise. With him, everything seemed possible . . .'

As the delivery of her words became faster and faster, what Lucile was saying (I can only relate the gist of it here) gradually acquired a strange capacity, washing my past like a sponge soaked with some processing solution. Events in my life were transformed, taking on a different aspect, a peculiar distinctness. If I had not known Dr Fohat, I might have thought, hearing his niece's enthusiastic description, that her love and affection distorted the picture she gave of him.

'A kind of perpetual transmutation shrouded his life with mystery. Of his work I knew only that he had run some big business, a doll factory, he told me. And he spent the best part of his time painting eyes for these children's toys. His prime concern having been to teach me this art, I spent all day long with him, engaged in this activity that was only apparently humble. My uncle prided himself on achieving an illusion of total reality when he painted these tiny pupils. He wanted them to have lifelike brilliance, and to this end he had become the inventor of products giving porcelain the transparency of the iris, the very depth of the human pupil . . .'

There was a brief silence, then:

'I forgot to tell you,' she concluded in an absolute rush, as if she had until then been concealing from me the most important part of her story, and had suddenly decided to reveal it, 'my uncle kept his promise. One night, a few days before he died, I dreamt that he brought me two splendid eyes, such as no little girl has ever had, and that he inserted them under my eyelids, without hurting me in the least . . . Was it only a dream? I don't know . . .'

And looking up at me, her limpid gaze innocent of all guile, she swiftly added, 'Aren't my eyes the most beautiful in the world?'

Shrill though the sound of her voice was as she said these words, while a grimace distorted her pretty face, it was unable to hide from me any longer the increasingly loud roar that rose from the depths, a sound with which nothing else interfered now and that we listened to, she with a kind of terror in her eyes, and I with uneasy surprise in mine. Having surrounded the palace, was the rabble now overrunning it? And yet there was something more dreadful about this approach than the successive chases that had left me defenceless, at the top of this peculiar abode. It was no longer the footsteps of multitudes hesitating in dark passages, nor the moving tide of a crowd encountering impassable walls, but a strong and irregular tattoo, the triumphant tattoo of an army on the march.

Before I had time to question her, Lucile was off again, dragging me in her wake, as if her mission were to lead me to places prepared in advance for me, that I had not known of and, without her, never would have, and of which she had been the faithful guardian since time immemorial. Despite my misgivings about the danger I sensed growing behind us, I took pleasure, as I had not been able to for a long time, in laying my hands in passing, and pressing heavily, on everything around me. There was no doubt, I was cured! The presence of this little girl, by immunizing my fingers against the spell on them, restored their true function and my use of touch. And I had lost nothing of my visual faculties! But the accumulation of wondrousness around me was slightly wearying my attention. Besides, I had eyes only for Lucile, whose pure and innocent face presently seemed to me the only thing that was tangible and authentic.

We had passed through the narrow doorway and were now running along a kind of ringwalk. As we climbed more steps to reach the terrace roof, it occurred to me to pick up Lucile, who weighed so little, and carry her. At my elation, she too forgot the imminent danger that only she knew the nature of. She laughed and I laughed with her. What fools we were! Although borne in my arms like the glorious burden of a conqueror, it was she who guided me! Ah, what did I care that she was the instrument of my redemption or I the instrument of her beauty!

What did I care that so many years had passed since my last interview with Dr Fohat, and that, through us, he should continue, from beyond death, to conduct an experiment of which we would never know the secret? Overriding the confusion of my thoughts there was at least this reality, this adolescent body that my hands could hug tightly. I clung to it as to a lifebuoy. But would that this headlong rush should cease! Would that this frantic adventure, which cast into turmoil my thoughts, feelings and memories, should stop! Lucile! My child with eyes of light, dispel the darkness in which I am floundering like a drowning man still thrashing about in the arms of his saviour! She consented to the kisses with which I covered her face, adorably feigning to defend herself against them. Yet, mingling with my keen pleasure was a sense of nausea I could not overcome, a feeling of disgust brought on by the speed of the moment, a dizziness caused by such haste, that robbed this happiness of all certainty.

The ringwalk led us, via a labyrinth of suspended stairways and platforms, over buildings separated from our point of departure by the width of the courtyard. The noise behind us had faded to an indistinct rumble that we sensed in pursuit of us. I had put Lucile down, and we walked hand in hand alongside the parapet protecting us from the drop. When we came to a narrow gap in the wall of the parapet that in all likelihood gave on to the void, my young friend came to a halt.

'This is the only escape,' she said. 'The main thing

is not to let THEM touch you . . .' Then, in the face of bewilderment, and as though she could not explain, she added hastily, 'Don't worry. You're with me . . . we're together . . .'

But the anxiety in her eyes contradicted these reassuring words. I was finally going to question her, ask her why she was trembling, when all of a sudden a wall appeared, around the terrace roof within our view, like a continuation of the parapet itself. This wall was alive. It was closing in on us, reducing the space around us. And in the utmost amazement, I recognized the very same statues I had seen massed together in the courtyard a little while ago, or ones that were absolutely identical. A moving rampart of iron, earth or stone (their substance, which in the light of dawn had looked like lead, under the glaring light on the terrace roof had the glint of steel), these automata, standing side by side, encircled us. No, this was no longer the crowd capable of feelings, of wavering in its hatred, but the ruthless jaws of a trap, the unstoppable roller of a machine.

Dumbfounded, unable to make any move to stop her, I saw Lucile walk towards these mechanical monsters (they could not possibly be living creatures!). Already they had surrounded her. I saw her slip between their columns and disappear, swallowed up by their closed ranks. They now occupied the entire rooftop of every building, as far as the eye could see. An eerie guard of this modern fortress, their silhouetted figures stood out against the sky on the opposite parapet. They invaded every nook and cranny with the precision of natural forces, as earth blocks a hole in space, as water holds to the recipient that contains it, as fire cleaves to what it devours.

These robots that I had taken for ornamental figures of human likeness when they were standing still, seemed to me, in motion, to bear only a vague resemblance to mankind. Shrouded in lead cloaks, they glided rather than walked on the surface of the ground, which explained why the rumble of their ascent had turned into this even more unnerving subdued hum. Their arms, with hands moving at the end of them that looked as though they were gloved in black leather, swung with slow regularity. Their heads, beneath a kind of large flat helmet, were of entirely human appearance in shape and motion, but a mask of the same dark elastic material covering their hands blanked out the features, leaving only the eye-holes. And in these holes gleamed two *live* eyes. The sight at close hand of these fantastic creatures, with a green sheen now cast over them by the broad light of day, filled me with terror. Preferring to break my bones rather than be crushed by them, I darted into the opening that Lucile had pointed out to me. A stone ledge projected out from it. Crawling on all fours above the void, I managed to get to the end of the ledge, from where there hung a kind of cabin. It was child's-play to slide on to the roof, lift open a skylight and drop down inside.

As soon as I was within those four walls, a great sense of security came over me. The space in which I found myself contained the necessities of life: a bed, chair and table. Oh, what a surprise! There were even a few boxes of Dr Fohat's pills on this table! I suddenly felt transported years back, to the little room in the square. But I was so exhausted that I made no attempt to elucidate this further mystery or to sort out the chaos of my thoughts. Falling on to the bed, I immediately sank into a deep sleep. I must have slept a long time. When I opened my eyes and was truly conscious of being awake, I wondered for a few moments what had become of Governor, of the quiet congested wharfs, and the river I thought I had dozed beside, after crossing it, the previous day. What was the significance of this narrow cot, these cramped quarters, this prisonyard lighting?

I got up quickly, and the moment I put my foot on the ground I experienced an unpleasant sense of instability which further increased my discomposure. There was no doubt, with every footstep the whole room, walls and ceiling, swayed slightly. I could not, as in the past, attribute this unsteadiness to an effect of my eyesight – it had regained all its sharpness – nor to a temporary dizziness. No, this sensation of gently floating clearly came from an infinitesimal rocking of the cell itself, caused by my weight on the floor. Having run across from one window to the other, I just had to admit the only plausible explanation for this phenomenon: I was in a moveable room, a kind of enormous lantern or suspended cage. And as I strove to comprehend how I had ended up here, recent events came flooding back into my mind in a sudden rush.

Was it not strange that I could have practically lost all recollection of them, that they should have been like the images of a dream it is difficult to reconstruct the sequence of after waking? Strange and terrifying! If this forgetfulness – this absent-mindedness – were possible, the day would come, after even deeper nights, when I would completely forget, beyond all hope of recovery, the whole extra-ordinary adventure of my dealings with Dr Fohat. For the time being, I had other worries on my mind!

Leaning out of each window in succession, I managed to determine my position in space. The lantern in which I was swinging like a flame guttering in the wind hung above the inner courtyard. No doubt, my excessive haste or the prevailing darkness had prevented me from noticing this lookout post. Then I recalled that Dr Fohat was dead, even though I was his guest in this abode (palace, barracks or prison?), but that his niece lived here. If it could only be true that she were still alive! In this cruelly burlesque, inexplicable world, this child who had so providentially appeared had become the only creature connecting me with immediate reality and at the same time with the memory of Dr Fohat. And the idea that she existed, that she drew breath, that she continued to move about somewhere within confines that were also mine reconciled me with my destiny.

Had the long series of vicissitudes before Governor's death been just a sequence of intermeshed, interlocking dreams within dreams? Two little living hands had recently woken me from this serial nightmare. Lucile! I must find her, and see her again, and not grow any more conscious of being awake! The army of automatons manning these walls were obedient to a will I would surely discover and vanquish.

Fired by these valorous thoughts, and after much

prying into every corner, I realized that the base of one of the windows opened, forming a doorway. Behind it, suspended above the courtyard, was an iron staircase. The distance separating the bottom steps from the ground looked an easy jump, and without further reflection I went rushing through this sole exit. But before I could appreciate my recklessness, the almost perpendicular angle of the staircase made me lose my footing. Sliding down from one step to the next, at first, without managing to save myself, I ended up tumbling all the way to the bottom of this booby trap, being made brutally aware of the entire futility of my enterprise. To cap it all, I thought I heard a great chorus of guffaws greet my fall. I had rolled into the middle of my guards who were falling about around me, overcome with mirth of which I could not but be the cause. Shame, anger and an inexplicable childish terror in the face of these jeering robots got me back on my feet. Without stopping to recover my breath, I retraced the entire route I had taken the day before, crossed the entrance hall, forgot, in my hurry, to take the lift, went panting up the staircase, came out on to the rooftop and from there, gasping, dishevelled, and aching in every limb, I set off at a run along the battlements until I came to the gap and slipped through it. Phew! I was safe! But I still had to do an extraordinary balancing act before regaining my precarious refuge via the skylight.

Every individual has the utmost freedom at every moment, wherever they might be, if they only keep hope. Just as before, in the small hotel bedroom, my only support had been the hope of better eyesight, my comfort in this moving cell was the hope of seeing Lucile again. How could I have remained in that prison for a single moment without hope? I would have asked myself that question as I entered it, and most surely fled from it, preferring, to isolation on this perch, to return to the world that mysteriously stopped at its threshold; preferring, to these silent barracks full of obscure menace, the envious viciousness shouted in the streets. But all I saw of this trap was the bait, that charming face momentarily upturned towards mine and those eyes that shone for me alone.

Was not this gigantic construction a larger-scale replica of the hotel where I once narrowly escaped being imprisoned for ever? All things considered, nothing had changed but my recalcitrance – my past recalcitrance having become whole-hearted acquiescence. But actually this acceptance meant that in reality everything was different, more terrible, more true; everything was new. And this happiness that my short-sightedness of previous years had made me scorn, when my sole concern was to find a cure, I now desperately wanted and desired with all my taxed and obdurate faculties, as if it were my due. Yet could it still be a question of happiness? The very concept of this word had eventually disappeared, faded away, like the name on the tombstone of one buried in a foreign land. The possibilities for anticipating this happiness were so derisory they should have taught me to despise it. No, it must be something else, which I had perhaps only to wait for, telling myself it would come.

'It always comes, sometimes without announcing itself, and the time always comes when you know it's there, for ever more.'

But this time had not yet come, nor the time for waiting and doing nothing. I had to continue to seek, to be active, to try and find out at least what this other thing I did not know the name of was called.

I had too bad a memory of my fall to risk taking the steep staircase any more. Whenever I wanted to go out, I preferred to go and come back via the sky-light. In doing this, I quite quickly acquired the genuine acrobatic skill I previously lacked. When first the silence, then the stillness outside, guaranteed my freedom of movement throughout the huge barracks (a calm that recurred irregularly, without my being able to discern the cause, when the automata became harmless once more, some lined up as though on parade, others frozen in niches in the facades), I would haul myself up on to the cabin roof, and clinging to the jib that served to suspend my lodgings, using my hands and feet, I edged my way to the gap in the battlements and got on to the terraces.

The first time I managed to escape in this way, I went tearing through every building till I was out of breath, calling Lucile, shouting her name, which was echoed back to me from the high ceilings. But the silence resembled that of underground galleries that have been abandoned after some catastrophe. The secret of this strange place and its peculiar

187

atmosphere eluded me. Subsequently, I suspected that some hidden place remained barred to me and I was determined not to despair of finding it. Yet weariness compelled me to slacken in my search and I was reduced to contemplating the inert robots without managing to solve the mystery of their movement. When I furtively set off again on my wanderings, I did so feeling the thrill and anxieties of a thief, as if creatures of my own kind slept within these walls.

The awakening of my guards, in obedience to some invisible signal, the dull clanging of their troops in search of me, forced me to return to the cabin, sometimes not without endless games of hide-and-seek. But I got used to these breathless dashes, just as an asthmatic gets used to his fits, knowing the process if not the remedy. A little skill and lots of agility sufficed to escape the implacable mechanical resurrection, to outwit them in their pursuit of me and in their dissimulations. More dissatisfied with myself on my every return, I reflected on these fruitless sorties and, increasingly annoyed at not seeing Lucile again, and lacking the answers she would have given to my questions, I strove to make greater sense of our brief encounter.

Matching her words to my own memories cast sudden light on them. But I often wondered if this was not simply the effect of my imagination. So as not to have to admit to my dealings with her uncle, when I next saw her, I worked up a whole story in advance. Certainly, her candour and good faith would

make these little lies easier for me. Since Dr Fohat
had always concealed from this child the scientific
researches that obsessed him, it was not up to me to
reveal his secret to her. Besides this secret was not
entirely revealed to me, any more than it was to her.
A wonderful optician to one of us, a doll-maker to
the other, what disguise had he not worn in the sight
of each person? Unaware of the former power of my
hands that her presence annulled, Lucile believed me
to be enslaved solely by her beauty. So, being prevented from joining her helped me to prepare for the
misconception that alone could protect our union.
That this union should come about was all that I
yearned for; I deliberately kept at a distance anything that might have revealed to me the reason for it
and what was behind it. Was it not determined by a
will other than ours?

I had evidence of this one day, when my escapade
brought me back to the entrance hall, as it invariably
did, on every occasion. I recognized it from the lists
inscribed on the walls. Tired of exploring vast rooms
to no avail, and having nothing else to do, I studied
the gigantic hieroglyph for a long time. All the names
once formed by these signs, like the faces I used to
brush past on the avenue or encounter in the vicinity
of the square, were for me indissolubly linked with
mystery. Brief incidents had given me the illusion
that I would eventually penetrate this mystery, understand the significance of my surroundings, as the
fissure of lightning in the sky reveals a blurred land-
scape. Then everything had fallen back into even
more obscure darkness. But just as I was about to

give up on seeing light dawn in this darkness, just as I was on the point of turning my back on this puzzle, I noticed – from paying close attention or through inattention? – in the centre of the jumble a character of abnormal size, an 'I', from which I began a vague attempt at reconstruction.

Trying to suppress visually the distraction of the surrounding mass, which prevented me from seeing clearly the only part that now interested me, all at once, in a sudden blaze of revelation, two words appeared before my eyes, two real names that seemed to me the key to the puzzle and plunged me into a kind of ecstasy:

LUC LE
ADR EN

I swiftly returned to my room to reflect on my discovery in all tranquillity. It could not be simply a curious coincidence that these two interlaced names were there, in the midst of this baffling confusion. Did they testify to some pre-existing order, or were they the first beginnings of an order yet to come? In any case, starting with these two names and reconstituting the thousands of other names surrounding them proved humanly impossible. This key was of value only to myself and Lucile, it enclosed us in our own prison, giving access only to our domain. Was it not profoundly significant, though, that the only two legible names should be precisely those of the two sole living creatures in this place?

Bearing in mind the multiple circumstances that had brought me into this hall, and the jinx that had been put on me, and the many occasions when, thinking I was being hunted down, I had run away, without knowing that running away was actually taking me closer to my goal, I came to imagine that for every one of the other names here whose letters were jumbled, there also existed somewhere, deep in some other mysterious crypt, a key that its owner had the task of finding. Or perhaps that every inhabitant of the square, every inhabitant of the avenue, had his name written up here, intertwined with that of his own destiny. But this destiny did not concern me, and would remain for ever obscure to me.

Everyone had to live out his own experience. No one could be of any help to anyone else. Perhaps the people I once used to come into contact with also had an evil capacity to overcome, a dreadful power, which they eventually renounced for ever, or — why not? — had never been revealed to them. And yet they should have gained a keener awareness of this power so that the meaning of their fate might become clear. It was because of this power and the curse attached to it that they should have run away, and kept running, succumbing to an awareness of their predestiny. But they had lacked the courage. Had they even wanted to? Had they not forgotten the only thing that distinguished them from each other, the extra curse in their constitution, to which they were rendered immune by their cowardice or their weakness?

In any event, hence, surely, from their despair, indifference or obliviousness, came the frenzy so often to be read on their faces. I was left imagining that all that survived of those marvellous destinies was a travesty: these heinous automata that brushed past me today, sad shadows or reflections who had lost their bodies of flesh, their spiritual mantle. My recollection of the distant past made me even more keen to dedicate myself to the sole task of self-improvement. I did not doubt that the inscription was a signpost pointing the way. But I wondered whether that abnormally large 'I', that towering vertical line, at once a link and an insuperable barrier, had been placed there to entwine our names symbolically, or if the cheating of a well-meaning hand, by removing this letter from another name a hundred times more formidable, would prevent its reconstruction for ever.

The seriousness of these reflections, not untinged with absurdity, my impatience for the revelations that I sensed to be imminent, and the strenuous efforts I had to make to enter and leave my lodgings caused me a great loss of nervous energy. As soon as darkness encroached on my refuge, I would fall into a regenerative sleep, a kind of plunge into nothingness, that divided up time for me. Yet I could not say how many days passed between my discovery of the inscription and the moment when I set eyes on Lucile again.

I was jogging through the vast barracks, having eventually persuaded myself that this would increase the chances of our meeting, when I thought I heard what sounded like the echo of my own footsteps behind me. Thinking that the automata were emerging from their inertia, I quickened my pace to get back to the roof terraces, but contrary to what usually happened, this noise, instead of getting louder, became so quiet – and yet so close – that it prompted me to turn round fearlessly. Lucile was panting to catch up with me. Every day, without knowing it, we had both been looking for each other, persistent bad luck preventing our encounter. At last I held her close to me! But I had hardly registered this when, like seas that start to rage round two shipwrecked people, from all the rooms we had just passed through rose the sound of genuine pursuit.

Quickly, we had to separate, to flee. And it was under such conditions every time – perhaps our guards spied on us in their sleep – that I saw again and touched, fleetingly, my sister prisoner whose name was linked to mine. Time would come between us, a heavy fustian thrown over our cry before it was uttered. During our rapid embraces, her tiny little face, with eyes closed to contain their joy, was like a stylized copy of Edith's, which had not yet faded from my memory. And these appearances, in their fleetingness, also reminded me of those of my landlady in the distant days of the hotel. But when Lucile opened her eyelids, I immediately found this comparison absurd.

No doubt there was too much darkness behind me for this sudden light not to let an indiscreet ray penetrate it, illuminating precisely that nook where so much crude wreckage, generally steeped in mire, still lay about. And when the light went out, although I felt a great tenderness at the fragility the darkness gave to this face, a desire swept over me to destroy it, to crush it like some defenceless object. Fortunately my hands no longer had their diabolical power! And I could lavish kisses on her brow and cheeks without fear, and forget the ghostly jetsam of my remorse, forget the unappeased shade of Governor, forget everything. Even though nothing is ever forgotten, even though everything is recorded, and everything has to be accounted for.

A miracle of imponderability, this happiness belonged to the realm of air. Lucile, with your arms knotted round my shoulders, your hair spilling like water through my fingers, your breathing gently slowing to synchronize with mine, Lucile, I was stealing all this, like the sick man at the window of a hospital room steals his extra oxygen from others. My very desire evaporated, burned in its own flame. Already I no longer yearned with the same ardour for possession of this virgin whose name had been linked, prophetically, with mine. The hurriedness and insecurity of our embraces made our febrile silence resemble that of the assassin who knows that the corpse, sole witness of his crime, still lies in the next room. Fleeing, going our separate ways, remained our sole recourse, the only way out. We had not a word to say to each other, no time to say a word, just the few frantic moments necessary to love each other, or pretend to.

I soon wearied of this game whose rules involved so much suffering. A new discovery was to lead me to turn my back on it. Our desperate embraces dried up the source of my desire, of which Lucile in her innocence seemed not even aware, and my sleep became daily more disturbed.

One night, having lain for a long while forcing myself to keep my eyes closed, I had to open them at an unaccustomed time. My little room was all lit up! Fearing a fire, I hastily got up and, from my observation post steeped in darkness, I saw that the large glass-walled room separated from me by the entire width of the courtyard was flooded with brilliant light. I could see what was going on inside there as clearly as if I had been close at hand.

A four-poster bed replaced Dr Fohat's table in the centre of the room. On the bed lay Lucile, looking very small and swathed in transparent gauze. I thought at first she was sleeping, but I soon noticed that the actual posts of this ceremonial bed – in reality, four automata (yes, indeed, it was no illusion!) – were moving towards her. They leaned backwards or forwards in turn. More of these stiff sentinels were lined up round the room, ready to obey the least gesture of the mistress of the place. And, confronted with Lucile's completely transformed appearance, with her fixed smile, lacklustre eyes, and unusually slow movements, the totally crazy idea came to me that, although of a different substance, she, too, no more nor less than her servants, was an automaton, a kind of insentient puppet.

All the details of this scene became occasionally blurred or else sharply defined, as if the swaying of my observation post operated the focusing of an enormous pair of binoculars fixed to my eyes. So it was that I eventually worked out what Lucile was doing: she was simply playing with her dolls. At times – several of these childish and grotesque objects scattered around her went some way to furthering my delusion – I saw her as part of that rigid little world. But this distant activity eventually became a complete blur. Lucile must have actually fallen asleep and the guards around her reverted to the immobility that had made me mistake them for bedposts. Then this scene, as though stereoscopically projected on to a tiny screen against the darkness, suddenly blacked out, returning me to my perplexed solitude.

The following night, and every night afterwards, found me on the lookout. I no longer felt the need to meet my little friend any more. Besides, unlike before, I now had to catch up during the day on the sleep that I lost, spending all that time watching at my window. My life once again underwent a complete transformation. During these long vigils, and despite the intensity of the darkness that separated us, I learnt more about Lucile's character than during our rare and rapid encounters. She could not know that I was spying on her, and this ignorance was a guarantee to me of the sincerity of her gestures. Yet her eyes often stared with abnormal insistence at the dark windows of the lighted room, as if she were appealing, through the layers of shadow around her, to some attentive and devoted witness.

When Lucile, rising from her bed, moved about in her transparent dress, no matter how often I told myself that her guards were dumb, unfeeling machines, I could not help envying them a little. They lavished attentions on her, just like extremely stylish valets, and but for their metallic cladding, the kind of helmet they wore, and the jerky ponderousness of their movements, the illusion would have been complete. She apparently ruled over them, doubtless on condition she remained confined in that room where her pastime never varied: she was always with her dolls!

I felt resentful, almost jealous of this faithfulness to a memory. For it could only be in memory of her uncle that she spent long hours in this way, under the eye of these bodyguards, making new dolls, dressing up others, manipulating them in all sorts of ways. How could she herself fail to understand the pointlessness, the childishness of this chore carried out in pious remembrance, out of cherished habit? If she had been content to play with the dolls of her childhood, without that gravity, that imperturbable seriousness, that false satisfaction that imbued her features, I would willingly have accepted it. But what was the good of making new ones? Who could possibly need dolls here? There were no more buyers, or orders.

Sometimes out of tiredness, she fell asleep at the table, her little head sweetly wrapped in her bare arms. Then after a few moments one of the automata, as though obeying its own will, approached her and carefully taking hold of her to carry her to bed, lifted her light garments up high, with no regard for modesty, and I could see Lucile's slender bare legs swinging in the air.

'She's asleep, she's asleep . . .' I said to myself, 'that man is just an unconscious machine.'

But during those moments I was unable to calm myself. So much so that I thought I saw, gleaming around her, the eyes of all the other automata lined up against the walls. Some nights, fever transformed my vision into hallucination. And there was Lucile passively submitting to be her guards' plaything, or the guards taking advantage of her sleep to undress her, to remove her arms and legs, to paint crude pupils on her closed eyelids, as they had seen her do to the dolls. These figments of my imagination, surely aggravated by the instability and remoteness of where I was, heightened the nervous tension due to my solitude.

For the first time I flirted with the idea of leaving this absurd imprisonment and everything connected with Dr Fohat's memory. It would be easy to break the circle of enchantment. Easy, too, to cross the courtyard, walk through the high-ceilinged entrance hall, pass through the gate, and run, keep running until I reached town, where, perhaps, those who had banished me would welcome me like the prodigal son. But my love for Lucile kept me in the heart of this artificial, inhuman world, as though on an invisible leash. And when I had to get a change of air at all costs, I restricted myself to climbing out of my box through the skylight, despite the late hour of the night, at the risk of breaking my neck.

The darkness made crawling along the jib dangerous, so I would equip myself with a sheet or blanket, wrapping myself inside it to deaden the effect of the fall should I slip off. It is possible that a more deep-seated reason prompted me to disguise myself as a ghost in this way. I must have had something in mind, something I would not admit to myself. For a long time, despite Lucile's assertions, I had doubts about Dr Fohat's death, imagining him, since my adventures in the avenue, to be endowed with im-mortality. Surely, he wanted it to be thought that he was dead so that he could get on with his work more peacefully. I suspected that he was hiding in a secret room in this city, which, from there, he directed as he pleased. Only he could be the controlling brain behind these robots, only he knew how they worked, and understood the reasons for their movement or immobility.

There was some reassuring purpose behind these conjectures: I could not bring myself to see this as a world left to itself, with no real intelligence, all a matter of impulse, of which Lucile and I might be the victims. It was even possible that my long per-ambulations, supposedly in search of his niece, had never been for any other purpose but to find him, to see him again, to hear him and speak to him. And now that the poor success of my explorations obliged me to accept the evidence of his death, by making light of a personal danger I strove still to deny this same evidence. It was a strange habit of mine, this perpetual trick of discovering the true motives of my actions when I could no longer do other than admit them!

Once I was in the courtyard, to which my foot-steps automatically led me, in front of HIS statue,

becoming a good loser late in the game, I was inevit-
ably compelled to admit what my shroud was for. My
qualms lost all justification: no one could see me or
hear me in this gloom where I did not even recognize
myself any more. This was surely the hub of darkness, the axis where all posing fails and ceases, the
centre where self-regard crumbles and shame denies
itself. These figures standing to attention in the shadows were not even dead men, or ghosts. Oh, I was
alone, quite alone, with no explanations to give, no
comment to make. Calmly, resolutely, I then climbed
up on the plinth, and as if throwing a lasso, cast the
thick blanket over the stone image of Dr Fohat. I
was distinctly aware of the full extent of my ludi-
crousness and buffoonery. But I also knew that the
whole world would remain for ever ignorant of this
performance I was putting on to give myself the illusion that this statue was not a statue, that it was
alive. Alive! And yet I still hesitated, for a long while,
before beginning to speak in a very low voice:

'My dear Dr Fohat . . . I'm delighted that you can
hear me at last . . . Here I am before you . . . tell
me . . .'

Once I was launched, there was no stopping me. I
went on like this, ever more earnest, ever more per-
suasive. But I was only feigning madness. The madman wants to proclaim the logic of his action,
whereas I only carried out mine in the certainty
there was no witness to it. It was entirely discharged
of its consequences. Besides, sometimes abandoning
the playacting that was supposed to convince myself,
I could not help lifting the blanket a fraction and,

without interrupting my appeal for one second, another voice inside me whispered with a peculiar little laugh:

'I know that I'm talking into space ... Don't think I'm deceived ...'

On one occasion when, despite – or perhaps because of – this irrepressible inward laughter, I addressed Dr Fohat with more vehemence than ever, a noise behind me abruptly halted my entreaty. It could not have been more of a surprise coming from the statue. My face must have turned purple in the darkness. Jumping down from the plinth on which I had been kneeling, I took a few steps towards a kind of scratching sound. And it was then that a human groan made itself heard, and so unexpected was it that, although barely audible, its accents completely rent the night.

I was at the door to the hall, and this hoarse moan seemed to rise from my feet. Cautiously I bent down. My hands encountered something soft, then arms, then a face. This could not be Lucile. Then I remembered the old servant who had opened the lift for me, on the day of my arrival. So many things had happened since then that she had totally slipped my memory. Yes, the woman lying there could not be anyone else but Dr Fohat's old servant, the one who used to bring him his bread and milk in the attic. By what miracle had she managed to live undetected within these walls?

As soon as she sensed my presence, she feebly uttered my name. At that moment I was able to distinguish her features and saw that they expressed great anxiety. She was now mumbling syllables whose meaning escaped me. Sliding my hands under her shoulders, I dragged her into the hall, but several times over this brief distance she begged me to flee, with the same intonation as Lucile, at our first meeting, when the robots were about to surround us.

A danger of the same order, a menacing change around us was indeed about to materialize. But now I no longer suffered the anguish of ignorance. A mere glimpse in good time of the device of which we might be the intended victims was all I needed to escape it. The concerted attention of a lucid mind must surely vanquish all this precision, all this soulless logic. Glimmerings of light were beginning to move across the walls of a thousand incomprehensible names, but there was no sense of panic in me. Like the old floor-scrubber of the past, this woman alone could dispel my anxiety. It was no mere chance that had laid her at my feet. Chance had never come into it. I had no right, nor the will, to desert her. Having got her to understand this, I managed to lift her on to my back, despite her moans and groans.

Why bother to describe the trouble I had to reach the roof terraces in this way, then to get through the parapet dragging this living burden after me, then to keep her balanced as far as the skylight, and then slide her down into my refuge! Once my exertions were over, I had already forgotten them.

As Dr Fohat's servant lay on the bed in my cramped room, slowly regaining possession of herself, I recalled that I had not found either my name or Lucile's, just now, in the midst of the thousands of characters aligned on the walls in the hall. The letter linking them must have fallen . . . But all of a sudden I saw that the hands of the old woman in front of me were fervently clutching to her breast some kind of flat ruler. And I instantly recognized the detachable 'I' that had fallen from the wall, the 'I' without which the very symbol of my union with Dr Fohat's niece no longer existed.

During the delirium that preceded her death, the old servant often mistook me for her master.

'Dr Fohat!' she murmured, her features suddenly becoming animated, and words interrupted by sobs escaped from her lips.

This delusion now and again infected me – especially when I learned that at the end of his life he had lived in the cell where we now were – and perhaps it was to this near total identification with him that I owed my comprehension of the full scope of his intentions. Or else the sick woman recognized me and then pronounced my name with the same intonation as he had in the past. From her conscious or unconscious avowals, which I laboriously pieced together, I managed to find out, little by little, no doubt more than she wanted to tell me. All became clear, as before in the lofty attic where I regained my eyesight, but nothing could dim the clarity of vision bestowed on me today, at the bedside of this dying woman, like the tragic awareness of the irremediable, nor liberate me from the profound despair it instilled in me.

For long-drawn-out days, like the shipwrecked

sailor writing an account of his shipwreck in the pressure cabin as it slowly sinks to the depths, the humble woman described to me her life with Dr Fohat. When her account merged closely with my own memories, I wished I could tear the words from her mouth. But she would often doze off then, and on waking resume her tale at a much earlier date. And I feared that the most recent events would elude me. From every new detail, however furtive and imprecise, I tried to reassemble the constituent elements of this lengthy experiment wrested from oblivion. I was impatient to know the last chapter of these memoirs before darkness reclaimed them, to put the final full stop to this diary of a dead woman. (I imagined that tombs must sway in the darkness of death as this room swayed, and that the dead often got up to feel the sides of their walls as I was doing . . .)

What kind of technical report can be given of the city conceived and realized for our use by the Doctor? We would need recourse to a science whose terms only he was familiar with. And anyway, it would exceed volumes. Comprehension of these things is beyond mere understanding, more the fruit of presentiment than deduction. I shall only try to explain — as it was revealed to me, listening to the sole witness to his research — the thinking behind this artificial paradise that was entirely fabricated to preserve Lucile and me from the outside world, and of which we were supposed to be the happy inhabitants, and when things began to go wrong.

When Dr Fohat died, the robots, those machines

of vaguely human likeness that caused my astonishment, had a degree of 'comprehension', if I may
use the word, sufficient to obey Lucile's every
thought, to comply with her least desires, and fur-
thermore to prevent any incursion from the outside
world into the domain that this modern demiurge
imagined he was creating for us. The names and the
way they were ordered in each list in the hall, which
constituted a kind of immense control panel, were
what guaranteed this obedience and the perfect func-
tioning of the whole system. But some time afterwards, it so happened that in some of the robots this
degree of 'intelligence' (of course, what we are talking about are solely 'mechanical' phenomena, but I
have no other words but those in my poor vocabulary
to try to describe these marvels) must have exceeded
the limit intended by their inventor.

One night an accident occurred. Abandoning their
duties, several of these domestic robots, independ-
ently of the young girl's will, and completely without
her knowledge, rushed out of the yard and into the
hall, where they had a go at the countless delicate
connections controlling their capabilities.

At that time the old servant lived in the suspended
cabin that had been Dr Fohat's abode at the end of
his life. An iron staircase – I had tried out the
remains of it, to pitiful effect! – then allowed easy
access to it. Every morning she would descend this
staircase to go and meditate reverently before her
master's statue. That day the abnormal activity of
some of the guards and the unusual atmosphere
prompted her to enter the hall, where she must have

found the Doctor's work partly destroyed. All the letters lay on the ground in an indescribable jumble.

Despite the impossibility of reconstituting the order of the names, which alone could have re-established the complete dependence of the robots, she had patiently applied herself to the task with the stubborn determination of simple souls. Little by little, she remembered her master's codings and by dint of her tenacity managed to prevent the destruction that would have left these robots to their own devices. Fortunately she recalled two names forming the centre of the panel, those two names – mine and Lucile's – whose single 'I' controlled one of the essential power units of this inconceivable operating system. But the disorder caused by the incident, having a tendency to reassert itself every day, demanded of the old woman its constant monitoring. By the time I arrived this surveillance was already partly beyond her. And fear of failing to respect her master's will by confiding to me her problems (what could I have done to deal with them?) drove her to continue in secret this exhausting battle against progressive disintegration.

She was to be defeated by it. Who or what was to blame? Perhaps everything that had delayed my arrival here? Yes, that must surely be the one flaw in this experiment. Dr Fohat himself should have imparted his instructions to me before he died. Now it was too late, even to save what was left to be saved. Instead of the all-powerful beings Lucile and I should have been, had we not become sad slaves at the mercy of forces unleashed at the expense of our happiness? The apparent harmony that had continued to prevail thanks only to the old servant's vigilance, at the loss of her unique and faithful attendance could cease to exist from one moment to the next and the wonderful system, breaking down completely, could destroy us.

As soon as I became aware of this, I hung even more anxiously on the old woman's words, I implored her silences, beseeched her to teach me how to continue her task. Not being addressed any more to a statue, but to a creature of flesh and blood, my entreaty acquired a force of sincerity never achieved before. Yet what weakness, what renunciation, in that poor body which was my sole recourse! Was the little of Dr Fohat's knowledge to which I could reasonably aspire to be conveyed to me through those delirious lips? The sounds that escaped them were increasingly rare. How wretched my hopes, how insane my aspirations! A whole lifetime would not have sufficed to learn how the robots worked, and I had only a few seconds that were being swallowed up by silence.

To go running, without tools, without arms, to the places under threat, to try to re-establish order where disorder was at every moment increasing – was this not the panicking of a frightened ant? Was it not, under the pretext of seeking to remedy evil, to run away like a coward from the very awareness of that evil which the dying woman's every syllable was instilling in me?

When that poor face had imparted its last murmur, the weight of the disaster that the Doctor's old servant had until that moment succeeded in preventing, perhaps by her voice, undoubtedly by her every second's devotion, seemed to fall on my shoulders, with the restored silence. But in the midst of despair lies profound peace. This fitful whisper from one close to drawing her last breath awakened in the most grief-stricken part of myself a new conviction that was to owe nothing to anyone else. It already glowed softly in my soul like a gleaming lake, a giant's sword in the depths of a dark forest.

Without ceasing during this long vigil to watch the lips from which emanated those illuminating words, I sometimes chanced to look towards Lucile's room. And I saw her extend her arms in my direction and cry out with all her strength, a cry that the density of the night prevented me from hearing. Looking up at my skylight, I had also seen silhouetted there – and there could be no question any longer of hallucinations – the aggressive helmet of one of the robots. I heard the multitudinous rumble of the storm gathering beneath me grow louder. Even then I knew that I had only to turn my eyes to see, so near and yet so far, the imploring figure of Lucile at the mercy of the monsters, calling to me through the dizzying shadows. But more powerful than all love and pity, more powerful than the anguish of fear, was the seed of suspicion, bred of the old woman's revelations, whose magnificent blooms of certitude were rapidly flourishing inside me.

If the power in my hands, the power from which I had been delivered by Lucile's presence, was not a mere figment of my imagination, suggested to me by

an ironic magician, but actually a 'terrible misfortune' that Dr Fohat had remained unaware of
right up to his death, this penalty for his experiment
was the only thing left that I could call my own, just
as their rebellion was all that the robots could lay
claim to. I had been operating in a warm limbo, full
of humidity, where everything was given to me, the
object of my desire and even my desire itself, but this
humidity was not mine. I suddenly felt revolted by
it. This embryonal environment did not belong to
me; naked, repulsive, wretched, but strong in the
young claws of my liberation, I had just broken out
of its shell. The power I believed to be pernicious was
my blessing and my strength. I would spend the rest
of my life trying to learn, by stern discipline, to gain
control of it.

Let the dawn, beyond these walls, break on the
grievous horror of a new world. Let this world keep
undergoing new metamorphoses every day, to scare
me. Let its multiple faces never cease to grimace. It
would remain powerless against me: my hands would
know how to protect themselves against each of its
manifestations, or destroy them. A flickering light
appeared at the bottom of my pit. This strange city
could prepare its torments and bury me under its
ruins, I would rise up to stride, light-footed, over the
rubble. Lucile's cries could travel through the walls,
her little fists hammer on the door, her running footsteps and sobs fill the corridors, I would thrust away
the smiling face of her love as though insulting the
execrated memory of one now dead.

Armed with this new harshness, as though with

armour-plating, I leaned out above the courtyard from which shouts rose, where lights flashed. And despite the presence behind me of the dying woman whose hand still scrabbled on the blanket as though to trace on it a final secret, it was actually laughter that distorted my features, gripped me by the throat, and shook me: wholly conscious of their freedom, the robots had overturned Dr Fohat's statue. It lay in the middle of the courtyard like a huge extinguished candle. And, by the glow of fireballs that some of them held aloft in their insensitive hands, they were now digging his grave.